Lock Down Publications and Ca$h Presents

HIDEOUS

A KILLER BY NATURE

Written By

TOMMY COOK

First Edition 2025

Printed in the United States of America

Lock Down Publications
P.O. Box 944
Stockbridge, GA 30281
www.lockdownpublications.com

Like our page on Facebook: Lock Down Publications
www.facebook.com/lockdownpublications.ldp

Stay Connected with Us!

Text **LOCKDOWN** to 22828 to stay up-to-date with new releases, sneak peaks, contests and more…

Like our page on Facebook:
Lock Down Publications

Join Lock Down Publications/The New Era Reading Group

Visit our website:
www.lockdownpublications.com

Follow us on Instagram:
Lock Down Publications

Email Us: We want to hear from you!

ACKNOWLEDGEMENTS

First off, I want to say thank you to the man above, all my blessing comes from you! Second, I want to thank my beautiful mama Jeannie Cook for always believing in me.

Jeremiah, Tommy Jr, Jamiyah, Paris, Kamiyah, and Ma'leah daddy love y'all so much. Y'all the reason I put these words together. Y'all the reason I go so hard.

My letter pad and pen is what get me through the lonely nights in this dark, waterless dungeon, but through the grace of God I persevere through it all.

To my fans, thanks for showing me love, spread the word about the new raw and uncut writer that writes with a message. I don't believe in writing fairy tales. I write what happens 24/7 in the streets. I keep it all the way one thousand with my readers.

ABOUT THE AUTHOR

Tommy cook was born and raised in Dallas, Texas. He was currently incarcerated in a state prison in Texas, where he decided to pick up a pen and letter pad. His style is raw and uncut.

Inside a prison is where he found his talent and with that talent, he vowed to keep it real at all times with his fans and readers.

Prologue

Friday morning

Hideous stepped outside, unaware of the chaos that was about to unfold right in front of the house he was left for dead in. It was a beautiful evening as he stood on his block. He headed across the street to fire up a blunt and when all he heard was the ear-piercing sound of tires burning rubber on asphalt.

He snapped his head in the direction of the car heading straight toward him. The driver was losing control of the red Dodge Charger. Lucky for him, he had enough time to jump out of harm's way. Good he did. The Charger made contact with a telephone pole.

"Damn!" Hideous couldn't believe his eyes. It was like something out of the movies.

The crash killed the driver and the passenger on impact, leaving Uzi Mi and his brother badly injured.

Uzi Mi was determined not to go back to jail. Badly injured and all, he still managed to climb out the window. He heard his brother's soft pleas for help, but he had to get the money right now.

"Help me, nigga! I'm yo' flesh and blood," Red Ronnie yelled out in pain to his younger brother.

"Hold up, nigga," Uzi Mi said, struggling to pull the duffle bag out of the rear window.

Hideous didn't know what to do, so he ducked behind a nearby bush.

When Uzi Mi finally got the duffle bag free, he could hear the sounds of sirens, and he saw the choppa again coming ahead fast. He quickly made his way toward the other side of the crashed Dodge Charger. He reached out a hand to his brother.

"I thought you was gon' leave me out here. Hurry up. I smell smoke." Red Ronnie groaned.

Uzi Mi looked and saw smoke coming from the engine. "I gotcha. First, hand me the other bag!"

Red Ronnie managed to hand him the other bag, not expecting what was about to happen next.

Uzi Mi looked back and saw red and blue lights in the distance. "Fuck!" He took off limping toward some nearby bushes. He stashed the money deep off in the trenches and made a run for it toward the opposite direction. He could still hear his brother yelling for help. He didn't even bother to look back.

The Charger busted into flames as he was being surrounded by DPD, and right then he knew all evidence was burned. All they knew he was the Uber driver caught up in some bad shit.

"The fuck you are smiling at?" A red-neck officer asked. "Where you're going, you're going to be there for a very long time!"

"We will see about that!" Uzi Mi spat before getting thrown in a squad car.

Once the coast was clear... Hideous jumped from the bushes with the duffle bags in hand. He watched as the last squad car left the scene, headlights disappeared in the darkness.

Twenties, fifties, and big face hundreds all stared back at him when he peeked inside one of the bags. The biggest smile spread across his face. He had easily walked away with seven hundred thousand dollars.

CHAPTER 1

Blood On My Hands

Scream had her face in a pillow, and her ass was in the air giving Yella Kid a perfect view of the colorful stars she had tatted all over her yella ass. She was throwing her ass back on him, causing him to grab her tiny waist. As she threw that ass back on him with extreme speed, she had to close her eyes tight and scream in the pillow.

SQUEAK! SQUEAK! SQUEAK!

Scream peeked over her shoulder to watch her ass smack off Yella Kid's stomach, but what she saw enraged her. "What the fuck!" She jumped up trying to cover her naked body.

Standing in the doorway with his iPhone aimed at her was Yella Kid's cousin Black Foot. He had been recording them having sex. *Shocked*, Yella Kid looked back and saw his cousin with an evil smirk written all over his chubby face. Yella Kid looked back at her with an evil scowl on his face.

"So, you knew he was recording us?" Scream asked with fire in her eyes.

"Yeah, bitch, I told him to. Now get yo' shit and get the fuck out before we decide to run a train on yo' slut ass!"

Scream stood there naked, ready to go in on his bitch ass, but instead she crossed the room, retrieved her clothes, and stormed out of Yella Kid's trap, feeling embarrassed.

Later that day, Scream was locked in her room crying, thinking about how stupid she was. Now the whole hood probably seen her sex tape.

Knock! Knock!

"Go away!"

"Open the door! Mama told me to come check up on you. She said you been locked in your room all day on a Friday, and that's not like you," he joked.

The sound of her twin brother's voice took some eased off the situation. She loved her brother more than anything and she knew he loved her the same. "Nooo, get the fuck away from my door!" she snapped, feeling her anger she had for Yella Kid and his cousin rise.

"Cool, I was just checking up on ya, but, bet."

She felt bad for yelling at her brother, so she unlocked the door and let him in. "I'm sorry. I just had a bad day, that's all."

Seeing his sister's red puffy eyes, he asked her, "You been crying?"

She put her head down in shame, covering her face with her hand, letting the tears flow freely. She hadn't cried in a long time, and for her brother to see her like that made him weak.

"What the fuck happened to you? Don't lie either!"

Scream knew her brother was crazy, and from what she had witnessed with her own eyes, he was a ruthless killer. She knew he would kill anybody that crossed her path. He'd proved that to her just a year ago.

One year ago...

"NOOOO! Reuben, you're going to kill him!" she screamed from the top of her lungs.

WHACK! WHACK! WHACK! WHACK!

Hideous was beating Scream's boyfriend to death with a metal bat, straight to the head. Hands tugged at him, trying to pull him off the bloody, unconscious Eric, but he shoved them away and swung two more bone-snappin' blows—cracking ribs, snapping spine. He wasn't done yet. He cocked back and smashed the back of Eric's head, busting his shit clean open.

After lying to her brother—telling him Yella Kid and his cousin had raped her—Scream knew the streets were about to bleed behind her brother's hands.

***

Yella Kid and three of his boys were huddled around the screen of his cousin's iPhone 14.

"Damn, that bitch throwin' that ass back," Slim Walk said.

"And you say that's the same Scream from that Kite DM magazine we sent Lil Cuda in TDC?" Ghetto asked.

"Can't you see the colorful stars all over her ass, muthafucka?" Yella Kid snapped.

"Ain't that… damn, what's that ugly ass nigga name that always be to himself? Fuck, what's his name?" Lil Man thought hard.

"Hideous," Yella Kid answered.

"Yeah, I heard they twins, but how the fuck that happen? He ugly as fuck and she fine as hell," Ghetto said, confused.

"And she yellow as hell while that nigga black like Michael Blackson off Next Friday," Lil Man joked, making everybody laugh.

"I heard that YN crazy like O-Dawg. Straight menace," Ghetto added.

"Man, fuck that nigga and his hoe ass sister," Yella Kid barked, restarting the video for like the tenth time.

***

Black Foot ushered two crackheads into the living room—one of them being Hideous, hood pulled low over his face.

"Bitch ass nigga, give me my phone," Yella Kid groaned. "Damn, how many times you gon' watch that hoe?"

Hideous clenched his jaw at the sight of his sister being smashed.

"Nigga, fuck you. And what these niggas want?"

"Oh yeah, they want a dime rock," Black Foot said.

"Where y'all paper at?" Yella Kid asked.

"Say, Slim Walk—go get that," he ordered without looking up from the phone.

"Hurry up and get that paper, nigga," Black Foot said, eyeing the crackheads.

"Hold up," the first crackhead said, reaching into his sock. He pulled out a sweaty dollar from one side, another from the other.

"Man, what the fuck? You can't help out yo' partner?" Black Foot asked, glaring at Hideous. But Hideous kept his head down, not wanting to be recognized.

"Man, look at this nigga. See, Ghetto? Leave them drugs alone," Black Foot joked.

"This nigga retarded or some?" Yella Kid spat. "Get this nigga the fuck out my spot."

What they *weren't* expecting was the carnage about to unfold.

Hideous slowly raised his head.

Locked eyes with Yella.

And without a word, he pulled a big-ass .357 from his hoodie pocket and opened fire.

At the same time, Crazy Red—the other crackhead—whipped out his .40 and started shooting at anything that moved.

BLOCKA! BLOCKA! BOC! BOC!

Black Foot dove for cover and saw his cousin laid out, half his face blown off. He bolted for the back door but

Hideous caught him with a .357 round to the back of the head.

When the smoke cleared, every one of Yella Kid's partners was dead.

Crazy Red started ransacking the house for drugs and money. Hideous picked up Black Foot's iPhone and pressed play on the video Yella Kid was obsessed with.

Seeing his sister being pounded made his stomach twist. He dropped the phone.

"*That bitch lied to me…*" Hideous growled.

A door slammed somewhere in the house.

"Hideous!" Crazy Red shouted.

By the time he made it back to the living room—holding a whole pound of kush—Hideous was gone.

"Damn, bitch ass nigga couldn't tell me he was leavin'," he muttered.

A loud moan from the phone made him look down.

"Oh fuck… oh fuck… right there… don't stop!"

His dick jumped.

"Damn, Scream… I ain't know you were a freak like that. I'ma have to see about you myself," he said, smirking as he pocketed the phone and walked out with a pound of Za and $3,200 cash.

CHAPTER 2

Sex Slave

An hour later...

After Hideous got back home, he went straight to Scream's room. Without knocking, he opened the door.

"Bitch, why the fuck you lie to me?"

Scream sat up on her bed, still lost in her brother's words. He had never talked to her like that.

"What the fuck are you talking about?"

"I seen the video, bitch. Why you still lying to me?"

"Get the fuck out my room. I ain't lying. I did get raped. I can't believe you, Reuben."

A knock at the front door interrupted them. Hideous rushed out, leaving Scream speechless.

"Bitch, we ain't done talking!" Scream blurted as she hopped out the bed and followed him to the living room.

Crazy Red turned to walk away when the front door suddenly snatched open. Hideous and Scream stood there, both looking mad as fuck.

"Why you leave and didn't tell me?" Crazy Red asked.

"Not now, bro," Hideous spat, turning to walk toward his room.

Crazy Red stared at Scream, and instantly his dick swelled. He'd been thinking about her the whole way over. Scream threw her ass from side to side, giving him a full view of her juicy booty. She had on boy shorts that read LICK ME across the back.

"Damn, girl," Crazy Red said.

Scream shot him the middle finger and kept walking. She knew Crazy Red had a thing for her, but Hideous would kill them both if he ever found out they'd been fucking around.

"Hold up, boo," Crazy Red said, making Scream stop with her back still facing him. He walked up behind her and grabbed a handful of ass.

"Boy, my brother would kill you if he saw what you just did."

Crazy Red stepped back and smacked her ass again, watching it jiggle.

"Damn… that's all you?"

"The fuck? Boy, don't play with me. What do you want? If all you wanted to do was play with my ass, you could've come to DG's tonight and threw some munyun on me. I know you and my brother robbed them fools too," she said, looking him up and down.

"Naw, we just handled business. But do your brother know you strip?"

***

Four months ago…

Crazy Red had just robbed a big-time dealer out The Grove and went to DG's to celebrate. He damn near lost his mind when he saw Scream giving a fat nigga a lap dance. She begged him not to tell her brother. She knew he would've shot the whole place up; he was crazy like that.

"*Hell naw!* And he better not find out because you promised you wouldn't tell him."

"What you gon' do for me?"

"The fuck you mean?" she asked, hands on her hips.

Trying to dodge the question, Crazy Red said, "You know who you look like?"

"Who?" she asked, already knowing who he *should've* said.

"Cuban Doll."

"Who the fuck is that?" she snapped, expecting him to say Big Latto like most people.

"The baddest rapper in the city."

"Oh, I heard about her," she said with a nasty attitude.

"But she don't got shit on you."

"Boy, whatever."

Scream turned to walk away, but Crazy Red grabbed her arm.

"Boy, what the fuck do you want?" she asked.

Crazy Red reached into his coat pocket, pulled out Black Foot's iPhone, and pressed play.

"*Oh fuck, oooh fuck!*" filled the room.

"Now that I got your attention," Crazy Red said. "Now you know what a nigga wants."

"You gon' play me like that for real? You know if my brother found out, he's going to kill you."

"*Fuck your ugly ass brother. You know the bizness. You know what a nigga want.*"

"So you gon' blackmail me over some pussy? You really gon' do me like that?"

"Bitch, you want me to make this video go viral? Or should I tell your brother how you be shakin' your funky ass for money?"

"Wow." Scream looked at her brother's best friend and shook her head in disgust.

Damn, look at this bitch's ass, Crazy Red thought as he followed Scream up the stairs to her room.

When they stepped inside, Scream peeled off her boy shorts and bent over the bed, naked from the waist down.

A short while later, after Crazy Red had busted all over her ass, he walked straight into Hideous's room. Hideous was lying on his bed, peacefully sleeping.

"Nigga, wake your ass up."

"Damn, nigga… how long I been sleep?"

"Not long. I drove Scream to the store. We just got back," he lied.

Hideous sat up and looked at Crazy Red with an evil mug.

"Nigga, you know I don't move like that. She's like a sister to me. I wouldn't disrespect you or your sister like that." Trying to change the subject, he asked, "Why you leave me back there?"

"Because, nigga, I was ready to go," Crazy Red shot back.

"You could've told a nigga! You left me in that bitch. What if the police had come?"

"*Fuck the police!* What you get?"

"Shit… they didn't have shit. And once you left, I didn't really have time to look," he lied again.

"Well, I'm 'bout to crash out. I'll fuck with you later today."

"Bet. I'll be over here tomorrow."

Crazy Red walked out of Hideous's room with a big smile, thinking to himself, *Round 2*.

Round 2

Crazy Red was behind Scream, stroking her with everything he had. It hadn't even been a full day, and he was already back inside her. Scream had her music turned up just enough to cover the moans coming from both of them. She prayed her brother would walk in and blow Crazy Red's top back, but she knew her brother slept hard.

"Lay on yo' stomach," he demanded between moans.

Scream stretched her phat, booty-heavy ass across the bed. Crazy Red licked all over the stars on her smooth yella cheeks. He eased a finger into her tight asshole, making her jump from the sharp pain.

"Nigga, what you got going?" she spat.

"This," he said, shoving his finger deeper into her asshole, forcing her to yell out in pain.

"*Nigga!*"

He fingered her with long, powerful strokes until her loud moans filled the room. Before she knew it, he was fucking her again—but this time deep in her ass. With a few more hard, driving strokes, Crazy Red nutted all inside her tight, juicy hold. Sweat had drenched him completely; his dreads were done for.

"Say, go get me something to drink."

After a long sigh, she sat up and reached for her boy shorts off the floor.

Crazy Red watched every move as she stepped into them, feeling himself, hands tucked behind his head as he watched her walk out the room.

Seconds later, Scream returned with a glass of orange juice and handed it to him.

He stood, drank the whole thing, and set the cup on her countertop.

"Take all that shit back off."

Scream frowned. "Damn, you wanna fuck again? What am I, yo' sex slave?" She slid her boy shorts down and stepped out of them, kicking them aside.

"Everything," he said in a serious tone.

She pulled her white T-shirt over her head, and her juicy titties bounced out—plump and round.

"Come here," he said.

She did as she was told. Scream climbed on top of him.

"For now on, you do what I say. You my bitch. When I say jump, you ask how high." He rolled her over and spread her legs wide before entering her as deep as he could go.

CHAPTER 3

Damaged For Life

Ms. Cash screamed as she watched flames spread quickly through her home. Her two young kids were still inside the burning house. She could hear her ten-year-old daughter screaming.

"*Somebody please save my kids, please!*" she continued to scream.

Neighbors, hearing her cries, began looking out their windows to see what was happening. The sight of the burning three-bedroom house was terrifying. Flames blazed everywhere. The young mother was numb; only a miracle could save her children.

"*Somebody, please! Please!*" she screamed again, tears streaking her face as she stared into the flames.

Suddenly, the front door swung open. Standing there was her ten-year-old son, Reuben. He quickly turned and rushed back inside, running straight through the fire.

"Reeeuubennnn!" Ms. Cash screamed after her small son.

Inside, Reuben could hear the frightened screams of his twin sister. She kept calling for help. He sprinted into her room, where she was hiding under the bed. The flames worsened by the second. Reuben grabbed her trembling hand, and the two dashed toward the front door.

Just inches from safety, the roof collapsed. The falling debris slammed onto Reuben, giving him just enough strength to push his sister out of harm's way.

"Noooo!" Rachel yelled.

"Go! Save yourself!" Reuben screamed in serious pain.

Before Rachel could react, a hand grabbed her from behind. She looked up to see her next-door neighbor pulling her out of the burning house.

"No, my brother! Please help him!"

"Sorry, chile… he's good as dead," the man said, staring into the flames.

The sight of her daughter's swollen, soot-covered face brought even more tears to Ms. Cash's eyes. She rushed to her and held her tightly.

"Where is Reuben?" she cried.

"He's dead, Mama," Rachel sobbed.

"Not my baby! Not my baby!" she yelled over and over.

"Look!" a man from the crowd screamed, pointing at the burning doorway.

Reuben had managed to crawl out of the burning house. "*Help me…*" was all he could get out before everything went black. The last sound he heard was his mama's fatal scream.

***

Six weeks after the fire

After the doctors did all they could, the entire left side of Reuben's face was badly burned, leaving him damaged for life. With half a face, his chances at a normal childhood were gone.

"Ewww! Look at his face!" a girl's voice yelled.

"*You freak!*" another voice shouted.

"*Damn, he ugly as fuck,*" someone else yelled.

"Who the fuck is that, yo' grandpa, Rachel?" another girl joked from behind.

"No! Fuck all of y'all!" Hideous screamed as he jumped up from his nightmare.

He replayed the traumatic memories—the fire, the teasing, the name-calling. All of it.

Reuben wiped sweat from his forehead and looked at his face in the cracked mirror. Rage rose inside him.

On the counter, Hideous picked up a photo of him and his sister at ten years old, just before the fire. He sat on the edge of the bed and stared at it, fury filling him again. Not a day passed where he didn't wonder if he would save her again… or leave her to burn.

After setting the photo down, Hideous stretched out on his twin bed and thought about the people he'd made suffer over the years.

***

12 years old

Mr. Anthony was down on his knees planting flowers in the garden in front of his home when a boy in a black hoodie approached him. Anyone else might've thought they were getting robbed, but Mr. Anthony knew exactly who it was. It had been two years since the fire.

"Hey, lil' man… how you been holding?" Mr. Anthony asked gently.

Reuben could feel his temperature rising. Ever since the fire, he had been filled with rage and hate. He'd wanted to hurt somebody—anybody—for a long time.

He pulled a .380 from underneath the hoodie he stole from his mama's boyfriend the night before. He aimed the glizzy directly at Mr. Anthony's chest.

"Hold up, son, it wasn't my fault!" Mr. Anthony shouted.

"You didn't even try to help me!" Hideous yelled, voice shaking with years of buried pain.

"Please… I have a wife and kids."

"And I got a fucked-up life," Hideous shot back as he squeezed the trigger.

BOC! BOC!

Mr. Anthony's body slumped to the ground. Unsatisfied, the young killer stepped over him and fired four more times.

A smile crept across his face as Mr. Anthony's body jerked violently.

BOC! BOC! BOC! BOC!

***

15 years old

"Reuben! Reuben! Wake up! Rachel out there fighting that lil' fast-ass bitch from up the street!" his t-jones yelled, standing over him. "Hurry up and get yo' ass up and go help yo' sister!"

When his mama left the room, Hideous jumped up and got dressed. He opened his top dresser drawer and grabbed his Glock. After checking it, he cocked it back and rushed out the door.

Outside, a huge crowd had gathered around Rachel and Fat Mama throwing down.

"That's who I been waitin' on—her ugly-ass brother," Mad Maxx announced as he bounced on his toes, shadowboxing. The crowd parted like the Red Sea as Hideous walked through.

A few feet away, Big Booty Susie was on the phone with her cousin Milky Way, Fat Mama's best friend.

"Bitch, hurry up—Fat Mama draggin' this hoe!" she lied. "Bitch, I gotta go—Mad Maxx just swung. You know this shit goin' on WorldStar!"

"Daaammnnn!" somebody yelled. "That nigga hit hard as a bitch!"

"WorldStar! WorldStar!" the crowd chanted.

"Fat Mama, at least pinch the hoe!" Susie yelled, holding up her iPhone as she recorded both fights happening at the same time.

Scream punched Fat Mama repeatedly in the face. She grabbed Fat Mama by the back of her weave and slammed her with punch after punch. Susie swung her camera to the other fight where Hideous cracked Mad Maxx across the chin with a powerful right hook that forced him to double over.

Big Booty Susie turned back just in time to see Scream stomping Fat Mama. Milky Way finally reached the scene and pushed through the crowd.

"I'ma fuck you up, bitch!" Milky Way spat, kicking off her flats.

"You not gon' touch my best friend, hoe!" Caprice rushed Milky Way, and the two hood rats started swinging.

"Oh my God!" Susie yelled. She handed her phone to someone in the crowd and ran to help her cousin. She pushed through the crowd—despite rocking a tight-ass dress with no panties under it. She squeezed in a few punches before Scream crept behind her and slammed her to the ground.

WHAM!

"Daaamnnn!" someone shouted.

The cameraman zoomed in on Big Booty Susie struggling to get up. Her dress was bunched around her tiny waist, exposing her naked ass.

"Damn, she got a phat ass booty," the cameraman said.

Susie finally got up straight. Her weave was in shambles, and both her titties were out, which made the cameraman zoom in even closer.

BOOM! BOOM!

Gunshots froze everyone. Mad Maxx clutched his throat as blood poured between his fingers. He dropped to his knees, then collapsed face-first in the street.

"What happened!" Scream shouted, taking an angry step toward her brother. "Reuben, what the fuck did you do?"

Fat Mama and Milky Way ran toward Mad Maxx, screaming. Blood pooled around his neck.

***

Before the shooting...

Hideous rushed Mad Maxx with deadly quick punches. He'd always been an experienced fighter, but Mad Maxx was skilled too. Hideous threw a fast jab, but Mad Maxx slipped it and landed a wild punch across Hideous's scarred face, sending him crashing to the ground.

Hideous looked up, breathing heavily, one hand squeezing the Glock he'd just drawn.

Mad Maxx stared down the barrel and laughed.

"What you gon' do with that, playboy?"

BOOM! BOOM!

Now Mad Maxx was choking on his own blood, tears running down his face. Fat Mama cried her soul out. Her baby daddy was all she had left after their newborn died at birth… and now he was dying in her arms.

"I don't wanna die…" were his last words before he died in his baby mama's arms.

CHAPTER 4

All Part of the Game

"Reuben, wake up, you sweating like a muthafucka," Scream shouted, shaking her brother by the shoulder.

"Damn… wassup?" He looked to the left at the clock glowing 1:30 a.m.

"Sorry to wake you, but you know rent due in three days, and Mama ain't gon' have the bread."

"So what?"

"Remember what we did last time to get the bread?"

Hideous let out a short laugh at the memory before he asked, "Yeah, but that shit was dangerous. I don't wanna put you through that shit again."

"I ain't ask you all that. I said do you remember. But I got another nigga we can get tonight. He at the motel waiting on me to come back right now. I told him I had to go get my homegirl."

"How much he got on him?"

"I know fo'sho ten bands… but he might got more."

"Hold up. Where you be finding these fuck niggas at?" Hideous asked, a concerned look on his face.

"He a Mexican named 2 Ton, and where else? Facebook, duh." She lied—knowing damn well she met him that night at the strip club.

"Let me call Crazy Red," Hideous said, reaching for his phone.

"Naw, I got my bitch already ready. She waitin' on us in the motel parkin' lot."

"Who, Caprice?" Hideous asked.

"Naw, nigga."

"Well, who then? The roommate you been talkin' about back at your school?"

"Naw… you don't know her."

"Why can't Crazy Red come? Why I gotta do this shit with a bitch I don't know?"

"Because she gon' be puttin' that pussy on 2 Ton while I sneak off to the restroom to text you when it's good. Damn, do you wanna get this bread or not?"

"Yeah… okay, let's go." He slid his hand under the pillow and grabbed his Glock. "I might rob that hoe too," he spat as he headed for the door.

One hour later – Motel 6, 2:45 a.m.

Molly's big ass slapped loudly against 2 Ton's body as she bounced back on him hard, trying to make him nut—but it only made him want her more. He gripped every handful of ass she had and met her with a body-shaking thrust each time she came back down.

"You get ready," 2 Ton said, licking his lips at Scream, who sat in a chair wearing nothing but a silver G-string lost somewhere between her massive cheeks.

I can't believe this shit. How am I gonna get out of this one? Scream thought as she stared at her dead iPhone.

"*Ahhh shit! I'm coming!*" 2 Ton roared as he nutted all over Molly's enormous ass.

2 Ton was a big 6'4", 250-pound Mexican who had just done twelve flat for murder. Scream glanced at the giant tattoo across his chest: P.G.V.

"It's your turn now, baby doll. Hold up—let me piss first," he spat, dick swinging as he walked toward the restroom.

"Damn..." Scream whispered, staring at his huge dick still standing tall. Molly jumped to her feet at the look on Scream's face.

"Bitch, what's wrong?"

"Bitch... my phone dead, and I don't know my brother's number by heart."

"What we gon' do now?"

"I don't know. You still got your pepper spray? I left mine in my locker."

"Naw... but I got my blade tho."

"Give it to me, bitch."

"Here." Molly dug through her purse and handed her a folded-up knife. Scream slid it under the pillow instantly.

Scream and Molly had met at DG's and been hitting licks together ever since. She'd even brought her best friend Caprice a few times. But this was the first time shit went bad.

A moment later, 2 Ton walked out of the restroom with a big smile.

"Damn, that felt good," he said, just as Molly slipped into the bathroom to clean the sticky mess off her ass.

"Damn, it stink in here," Molly yelled, slamming the door behind her.

Scream stared at 2 Ton with disgust.

"What? Baby, it had to be them Fuel City tacos I had before I got here." He sat next to her on the bed. "But enough talkin'. I been wantin' you all night," he whispered, sliding his huge hand between her thighs.

"Wait... I hope you got another condom," she said, praying her brother would kick down the door.

"I'm tryna get off in dat ass."

"What the fuck, nigga—hell naw. That's gon' be extra."

2 Ton reached for her G-string and ripped the flimsy material right off.

Scream gasped. He had just torn her favorite panties. That wasn't part of the plan—she *never* got naked for a trick. The licks always went smooth.

"That's gon' be extra. What you don't understand?" she snapped, staring at her torn G-string in his hand.

Molly came up behind 2 Ton and rubbed his broad shoulders. "You can fuck me in my ass, baby," she whispered to him, giving Scream a look to say *'Bitch, you owe me.'*

"Naw, I want her," he shot back, knocking Molly's hand away.

"Well, fuck you then."

"What the fuck you say to me, bitch?" He stood face to face with her, looking down with an evil scowl written on his face.

"You heard what the fuck I said."

BOOM!

He punched her hard in the face, knocking her the fuck out.

"What the fuck!" Scream yelled, reaching for the knife, but 2 Ton quickly grabbed her by the legs and pulled her to him. He flipped her onto her stomach and rested his horse dick in the center of her ass crack.

"Wait, I got to see if she still alive!"

2 Ton ignored her cry for mercy, and suddenly he pulled her back by her hips. He lined his dick up to its target and *Wham!* With a powerful thrust he was inside her tight ass.

"Oh my God!" She opened her eyes wide; the pain was too much for her to bear. She tried to run, but 2 Ton's grip was too tight on her small waist. Her ass was on fire from the intense pounding 2 Ton was giving her tiny hole. "I'm cumming." Scream's booty bounced to 2 Ton's hard thrust.

He fucked her ferociously. He drove his dick so deep into her ass that his dick was buried deep off in her.

"Shit! You got me cumming like crazy!" she screamed, grabbing the sheets tight as he upped the tempo, pumping her faster and beating her ass in.

"Unnghh… It's too much dick. You got me shaking!" Scream cried as her juicy ass cheeks splashed like a tidal wave.

2 Ton continued to hammer into her ass. She yelled from each brutal impact. He grabbed her jumping titties and pumped in her like a madman.

"Grrrrrr!" 2 Ton roared, shooting a thick load in her tight ass hole. "Damn, you two bitches earned this money. Sorry about knocking this bitch out," he spat, stepping over a stilled knocked out Molly.

He pulled out two big knots of cash from his pants that were laid across the chair. When he turned to hand Scream the money, she rushed him with a knife. Before he could protect himself, she stabbed him in the neck repeatedly.

"*Aaahhhh*!" 2 Ton yelled as Scream pushed the knife deeper into his neck, causing him to fall to his knees with blood oozing from his neck.

BOOM!

A few minutes later, Hideous burst through the front door to find a fat booty black bitch laying face-first on the floor next to a blood-soaked Mexican who looked to weight a ton.

Scream was counting out $16,000 from 2 Ton's pocket plus the 10-bands she had laid on the table.

"What happened? Why you didn't call me? I was worried about you."

"Everything good. Look, I got the bread. Now let's go."

"Hold up, did you fuck—"

"*What, fuck him*?" Scream shot back with her arms now folded across her chest.

"Yeah?" Hideous asked.

Scream threw her hands on her hips. "I got the money; that's all that should matter. Now help me with her."

Hideous pointed his Glock at the back of Molly's head.

BOC!

Scream forced out a loud scream in shock. "What the fuck wrong with you, Reuben? She was still alive."

"I had to make it look like a robbery. Or do you want to go to jail for murder?" A sly smile crept onto his face as he picked up the bloody knife.

Back In Scream's Room

Scream laid on the bed thinking about all the shit that transpired tonight.

"Molly, I'm so sorry," she whispered softly as she stared up at the ceiling. She closed her eyes and thought about the knife going deep into 2 Ton's neck and the way his bloody body sent a chill down her spine. She quickly reopened her eyes, not wanting to feel remorse. He was somebody's son, but he was gone. She couldn't redo what happened.

All for $26,000. She knew one thing; it was all part of the game. She had never killed anyone before. She wasn't a killer like her twin brother, but she knew if she had to kill again, she would.

CHAPTER 5

Lucky You

Next day...

BLOCKA! BLOCKA! BLOCKA!

"*Everybody, this a robbery!*" Uzi Mi yelled as he busted through the bank doors first. He grabbed the security guard standing near the entrance and shot him in the kneecap.

BLOCKA! BLOCKA!

Before any employees could scream, Red Ronnie, Bullet Head, and Gorilla Glock jumped the counter. Red Ronnie shot the closest teller in the stomach at point-blank range. The woman stared down at her hands, covered in her own blood, frozen in shock.

Screams filled the bank, but Uzi Mi waved his gun and fired into the air.

BLOCKA! BLOCKA! BLOCKA!

"Hurry up! We got less than thirty seconds!" Uzi Mi yelled over his shoulder.

Red Ronnie and Bullet Head emptied the drawers with quick, practiced movements, stuffing money into duffle bags while Gorilla Glock aimed his gun at the bank manager.

"Hurry up and get this vault open already," he barked at the petite white woman.

"It's open! It's open! Pleas—" she started before Gorilla Glock smashed her in the face with the gun. She hit the floor hard, and he stepped over her.

"Let's get this money," he spat.

Red Ronnie and Bullet Head followed him inside the vault and loaded every bag they had.

"*Let's go! Let's go!*" Uzi Mi shouted.

All four men bolted through the doors. As soon as they hit the parking lot, the silent alarm began to wail. Gorilla Glock jumped into the driver's seat of the stolen Dodge Charger. Bullet Head slid into the passenger seat while Red Ronnie and his younger brother, Uzi Mi, jumped in the back.

"Hell yeah… hell the fuck yeah! That's how you rob a muthafuckin' bank!" Red Ronnie shouted as they sped off.

SKIIIRRRKKK!

"Hell yeah," Bullet Head agreed. "Hold up, look!"

As they approached I-30, they saw a swarm of police cars flying down the opposite side of the freeway toward the bank.

"Just be cool. Nobody seen what car we hopped in. Chill," Red Ronnie said.

"The car stolen tho, bro. I can't go back to jail," Uzi Mi snapped, gripping his gun like a scared kid clutching a teddy bear.

"Hold up. See, I told y'all they were gon' come back for us."

"What?" All three men looked behind them and froze. One police car busted a U-turn… then all the others followed.

"I can't go back to jail," Uzi Mi repeated.

In seconds, a dozen squad cars were on their tail—and a helicopter overhead.

"Turn on this street, muthafucka! See can we lose these bitches," Uzi Mi yelled.

"I'm tryin'! Damn, I'm tryin'!" Gorilla Glock weaved through traffic like a professional stunt driver.

"Slow down, bro. Don't kill us," Red Ronnie pleaded.

"Fuck dat! I'm not goin' back to jail!" Uzi Mi shot back.

***

Hideous walked through the house—not the burned-down one from his childhood, but the new one the neighbors helped build. It sat right across the street from the ashes of the old home.

The house was a mess, just like it was the other night. Dishes piled high in the sink. A Williams Chicken box left open with bones everywhere and a half-eaten roll inside.

His t-jones and a thick woman sat at the table like the mess wasn't right in front of them.

"Boy, where the fuck you think you goin'?" his t-jones asked.

"On the porch to smoke."

"You got some dirty ass dishes in there."

"I got 'em. Let me relax my nerves first."

"Where yo' sister go? She left with that fast-ass bitch Caprice."

"I don't know. I don't be gettin' all in her business like that, Mama."

He had a crush on Caprice since middle school, but she never paid him any mind—not with the scars the fire left behind.

He stepped outside, unaware of the chaos about to unfold right in front of the house he almost died in. It was a beautiful evening. He crossed the street to spark his blunt near the old foundation—when the ear-piercing scream of burning rubber cut through the air.

He snapped his head up just in time to see a red Dodge Charger losing control, fishtailing straight toward him. He jumped out of harm's way right before the car smashed into a telephone pole.

"Damn!" Hideous whispered. It looked like something straight outta a movie.

The crash killed the driver and passenger instantly. Uzi Mi and Red Ronnie were still alive… barely.

Uzi Mi, bleeding and shaking, wasn't thinking about pain—only about prison. He forced himself through the window, ignoring his brother's cries.

"Help me, nigga! I'm yo' flesh and blood!" Red Ronnie yelled, voice trembling.

"Hold up, nigga," Uzi Mi grunted, fighting to pull the duffle bag free from the backseat.

Hideous ducked behind a bush, watching everything unfold.

When Uzi Mi finally freed the bag, he heard sirens screaming closer. The helicopter spotlight reappeared overhead.

He limped to the other side of the wreck to reach his brother.

"I thought you was gon' leave me out here… hurry up! I smell smoke," Red Ronnie groaned.

Uzi Mi saw flames licking out of the crushed engine.

"I gotcha… firsthand me that other bag!"

Red Ronnie pushed the second bag toward him—not imagining what would happen next.

Uzi Mi glanced back and saw red and blue lights flying toward them.

"Fuck!"

He limped off toward the bushes, stashed both bags deep in the vegetation, then took off running in the opposite direction. His brother's screams echoed behind him… but he never looked back.

The Charger burst into flames as DPD surrounded the scene. Evidence melted in the fire.

"The fuck you smilin' at?" a red-neck officer barked. "Where you're goin', you gon' be there a long time."

"We'll see about that," Uzi Mi spat as they threw him into the squad car.

Once the coast was clear…

Hideous jumped from the bushes with both duffle bags in hand. He watched the last squad car disappear down the block.

He peeked inside one of the bags—twenties, fifties, big-face hundreds stacked thick.

A smile stretched across his face. He had just walked away with seven hundred thousand dollars.

Back in the house, he crept quietly to his room. He could hear Scream and Caprice laughing. He peeked into his sister's room.

"Damn," he whispered.

Scream and Caprice were reenacting a Cardi B routine from one of her freak videos. Both women were on all fours. Caprice's ass bounced—one cheek at a time—making that thing jump. Hideous eased away from the door.

In his room, he shut the door, swept everything off his bed, and dumped all three bags onto it. His eyes widened—this was more money than he'd ever seen in his life.

Without knocking, Scream and Caprice barged in.

"Damn, Scream!" Hideous yelled, snatching a sheet to cover the money—but it was too late. Both women had already seen it.

"Where you get—oh my God!" Scream gasped. "You robbed that bank today. It's all over the news!"

"Hell naw. Ask Mama. I was here all day."

"You a lie. Mama was worried about you."

Hideous cut her off. "Can you please get out my room? I'll tell you everything later. I promise."

"I'm just sayin' what Mama said."

"Rachel… please."

"Okay." She sighed and walked out. Caprice lingered, staring at the covered-up money.

"Caprice… come on."

She tore her eyes away from the bed and followed Scream out.

Hideous hid the money the best he could. He walked over to his cracked mirror and stared at his broken reflection.

For the first time since the fire… he smiled.

CHAPTER 6

All The Way Turnt Up

Three days later

Hideous ran his tongue over his new forty-thousand-dollar 1/1 invisible set with emerald accents. His diamonds literally looked like a glacier. He could finally afford all the things he couldn't before. He was turnt all the way up.

He didn't know what to tell his sister, and he didn't want to lie, so he kept quiet. But she stayed on him — asking a million and one questions.

"Well, where did you get the money?" Scream asked.

"I don't wanna speak on that right now."

"You can't hide that money from Mama. She gon' see yo' mouth. You know how she is."

"I'm 'bout to get my own spot anyway, so it don't really matter."

"Really? Well, you better do something. And ever since that gold-digging bitch seen all that money, you are all Caprice talks about. At first, she couldn't stand you."

"Oh really?" An evil smile crept across his face.

Later that day

7:27 p.m.

As soon as Hideous left again — spending money like crazy — Scream laid back on the leather couch watching her favorite show *BMF* when her phone rang.

"What!" she snapped after seeing the caller ID.

"What you got going?" Caprice asked.

"Just sitting here watching *BMF*."

"Where your brother?"

Click.

Scream giggled, wishing she could've seen her best friend's face. She was tired of Caprice suddenly caring about her brother now that he had money. Before she saw him with a bag, she didn't give a damn about him.

Minutes later, just as Scream was sinking back into her show, the doorbell rang.

"I know Caprice didn't come to my house."

When Scream swung the door open she was ready to go off — but Crazy Red was standing there instead.

"My brother ain't here," she said with attitude.

"I'm not here for him," he said, stepping closer. He kissed her neck and slid her short boy shorts off, tossing them behind her.

***

Crazy Red sat on Scream's bed for a few minutes, admiring her juicy booty and the pretty face that matched her high-yella skin tone.

"What the fuck you smiling at?" she snapped.

He was about to answer when loud music blasted outside.

"Who that be?" he asked.

"You act like I fucking know!" she shot back.

"Bitch, don't get fly with me. This yo' muthafuckin' house?"

"And?"

"Bitch, shut the fuck up," he barked, peeking through the blinds. "What the fuck… I know this nigga didn't."

When Hideous pulled up in front of his t-jones' crib, he cut the engine, making Zee the Wizard's *Boss Nigga* stop blasting from the two 15s he'd installed just hours earlier. He hopped out of his brand-new black-on-black Cybertruck.

When Hideous stepped inside, Crazy Red stood up from the leather sofa and stuck out a fist.

"What's good, fam? When you get the new Cybertruck? That hoe clean as fuck," Crazy Red said.

"What you doing here?" Hideous raised an eyebrow.

"Scream let me in. I came to see why you ain't fucked with yo' boy since we got at Yella Kid and his niggas," he lied, eyeing Hideous's new Cuban link that spelled *Hideous*.

"Damn… that chain killing something."

"Nigga, get off my dick."

Who this nigga think he talkin' to? Crazy Red thought, remembering how he'd just had Scream bent over minutes ago.

"Nigga, put me on. Real talk."

"That's what I need to talk to you about."

"Okay, nigga. Talk."

"Follow me," Hideous said, leading him to the back room.

Crazy Red's eyes almost popped out his head when Hideous showed him four saran-wrapped pounds of weed.

"Nigga, what you on?" he yelled, excited.

"I need yo' help moving these hoes. I got six more put up. I'm trying to flood the streets."

Crazy Red was only nineteen — one year older than Hideous. With ten pounds, he could quadruple the little money he had. By twenty, he could be a self-made millionaire.

"When do I start?" he asked with a Kool-Aid smile.

"Now," Hideous replied.

"Bet."

"Take them four pounds, and remember… we only slangin' weed. If you buy anything other than weed, I can't fuck with you. Before I go to jail and get treated worse than a dog, I'ma have my court date on the streets," Hideous vowed.

Crazy Red nodded quickly.

"I'm also thinking about opening a strip club."

"For real? What you gon' name it?"

"Tipz," Hideous said, flashing diamonds.

***

Over the next few weeks, Hideous and Crazy Red were making serious paper. Hideous's plug was now giving him a hundred pounds of weed a month.

As the money came in, Hideous was still considering opening Tipz. He was flying down I-35 North with Crazy Red's Maserati behind him when he spotted a building for sale. It looked perfect for a nightclub. He exited at Regal Row and pulled into the empty lot, parking beside Crazy Red.

"This it right here," he said.

Crazy Red hopped out and walked the property with his boy.

After giving the seller what he wanted, Hideous walked out the new owner.

***

An hour later, back at his t-jones' crib, one thing was certain: he needed some pussy. He was eighteen and still a virgin — something he never told anyone, not even his twin.

When Hideous and Crazy Red walked inside, Scream and Caprice were on the couch smoking a fat blunt.

"Where's Mama?" Hideous asked.

"At work," Scream replied.

"Hey, Reuben," Caprice said.

He knew Caprice only wanted him for the money… but he only wanted her for one thing too.

"Come smoke with me." Hideous pulled out a blunt.

Caprice got up so fast she looked like an Olympic sprinter.

"Damn, bitch," Scream joked. "You ain't even got no money yet and already doing the most."

"Bitch, don't play," Caprice snapped — but Hideous had already pulled her away. He was trying to get his first piece.

CHAPTER 7

Too Many Lies & Secrets

Early the next morning
7:25 a.m.

Hideous woke up and shook his head at Caprice's naked body laying next to him. He was no longer a virgin, and by the way Caprice was screaming you would have thought he was a professional porn star.

As soon as she felt him getting out of the bed, she grabbed him by the hand. "Where you going?" she asked.

"Chase this money," he replied.

"What time is it?" she asked.

"7:25 in the morn," he responded.

"Damn, baby, you put a bitch to sleep?" She smiled. "Come back to sleep with me."

"I can sleep when I die."

He tried to get up, but Caprice grabbed his dick and began to stroke it slowly with her soft hands, and for the second time she was amazed at how big and thick it was. She took one last look before she made it disappear in her mouth.

7:45

Hideous stepped in the living room only in his boxers to find his sister watching TV. "Good morning, Baby girl."

Scream looked at her brother with a disgusted look. "Boy, you need to go put some clothes on. Mama in the kitchen with Ms. Parker. You do remember what happened last time you was half naked." She laughed.

Hideous chuckled. "Ms. Parker here? I remember. She was mad as hell, thinking I fucked on her daughter."

"Hell yeah. Mama still mad at you for what you did to her and Ms. Parker's relationship as friends," Scream mumbled.

A year ago...

"Reuben, I'm 'bout to take my shower. Sarah want for you to come and keep her company," Scream said with a wink. She knew that her T. Jones' best friend's daughter liked her brother.

"For what?" he asked confused.

"Nigga, I don't know. Go and see," she said walking out the room.

Hideous turned his head to the side and stared at his face in the mirror. He hated what looked back. On his way out, he punched the mirror so hard that it split down the middle. Even though it's been years since the fire, he still wasn't comfortable with his appearance. He vowed to never smile again, which he hadn't in years.

"Reuben, what was that?" Scream yelled from the bathroom.

"Nothing!"

"I know you didn't break another mirror! Mama gon' beat yo' ass!"

He shook his head. That was the sixth mirror he had broken just in that year alone, not counting the ones he had broken over the years.

He climbed a flight of stairs and entered Scream's bedroom. Sarah was sitting on the bed with her back to him, so she didn't know he had entered the room. He watched as she pulled her tank top over her head.

"Rachel said you wanted me," he said in a real low voice.

The sound of his voice startled her, causing her to jump. "Boy, you scared me." She chuckled, not trying to cover her bare chest.

"My bad, ma," he said, staring at her bouncing titties.

"Come lay with me," she replied seductively, biting on her pinky.

He climbed into the bed and lifted the sheets. He was surprised to see she wasn't wearing any panties. "Why you like me for?"

"I always liked bad boys, and plus my mama always kept me on lock down, trapped in the house. But fuck her. It ain't like I'm a virgin."

"But why me?" Hideous turned his head to the side.

"I just told you, Reuben." She grabbed him by the chin and turned his face so he could face her. "I like what I see. Rachel told me how you saved her life when y'all was younger. She said you her hero." She rubbed her hand across his burnt face, causing him to grab her hand in a kung fu grip.

The expression on his face changed from a frown to a mean mug.

"Ouch! You are hurting me, Reuben," she cried.

"Don't never touch my face!" he spat with venom in every word.

"I'm sorry." She leaned over and gave him a kiss, pressing her perky nipples up against him.

Hideous slipped his hand between her legs and stuck his middle finger in her wetness. "Damn, you wet," he whispered as her breathing got heavier.

She squirmed under his command. He moved his finger in and out of her soaked pussy with rapid speed.

She placed her hand on top of his.

"Just put it in," she gasped on the verge of an orgasm.

Still being a virgin, Hideous was a little nervous at what was about to happen, but his eagerness made him drop his

Jordan basketball shorts and boxers. Sarah was shocked at the length of his dick.

He quickly lay between Sarah's legs, and just when he slid the tip of the head in, he quickly pulled away.

"What's wrong?" she asked, confused.

"You don't hear that?"

"Hear what, baby?"

"Be quiet and listen." Hideous held his finger to his lip, indicating for her to be quiet.

"Ms. Parker, my mama is at work. I don't know where Sarah went!" Scream shouted.

"Bullshit, she said she was coming over here to fuck with you. Now where is my daughter?" After frantically searching the house for her daughter, she instantly became disappointed. "Where is your brother?" she asked.

"He's not here either."

Ms. Parker rushed past Scream, climbing up the stairs two steps at a time. "My daughter bet not be nowhere near yo' ugly, bad ass brother!"

"Please, don't call my brother out his name."

"Fuck yo' ugly ass brother! The whole hood knows he killed poor Mr. Anthony. I hope they lock his ugly ass up!"

"My brother didn't kill yo' sugar daddy."

"That's some fucked up shit to say to somebody that saved yo' life."

"My brother saved me— the fuck!" Scream vented.

Ms. Parker was first to make it upstairs. She walked inside Hideous' room to find it empty.

"Oh my God, my mama going to kill me. What are we gonna do?" Sarah mumbled, searching for her clothes.

"Let me handle this; I gotcha." With a smirk on his face he moved by the door and locked it.

Scream tried to open her door, but it was locked. She knocked lightly. "Reuben, open the door; hurry up," she whispered.

When Ms. Parker came out of Hideous' room, she saw Rachel with her ear pressed against her bedroom door. "Bitch! Move out the way!" Ms. Parker snapped.

BOOM! BOOM!

She banged on the door hard enough to break it. "Open this muthafucin' door, bitch!" Not receiving a quick enough response, she started kicking the muthafucka as hard as she could.

BOOM! BOOM!

"Damn! You gonna break my door! *Stop*!"

After she tired herself out, Hideous emerged wearing only his boxers with a big, evil smirk on his face. "Why you so mad?" he said, swinging his dick from left to right, causing his twin to cover her eyes.

Ms. Parker looked from Hideous' dick then averted her eyes to her half-naked daughter. She completely lost it. "Bitch, you up in this bitch laid up with this ugly ass nigga. You couldn't do better than him? Is you fucking desperate?"

Hideous stood there and watched as Ms. Parker beat the shit out of her daughter. He felt sorry for her. She was on the floor balled up as her mama punched and stomped her. All Hideous and his sister could do was laugh. That was their last time ever seeing the two of them again for a long time. Sarah moved in with her old man and Hideous went back to thugging.

Hideous shook his head at the memory. He was attempting to roll a blunt when he heard Ms. Parker's raspy voice.

"Okay, girl, I'm going to call you later," she said, entering the living room where Hideous was rolling up a pretty nice size blunt.

Ms. Parker moved behind the sofa and softly caressed his shoulders. "Come to my house later tonight. We can smoke and have some fun." She kissed the back of his neck that sent a shiver up his spine.

He knew Ms. Parker was known around the hood as a gold digger. Word on the block was she used to be a Playboy model when she was young and beautiful, but a hard life had aged her over the years. She still had her main money maker— her fat ass booty that could put Cardi B to shame.

That shit don't make no damn sense, he thought to himself. She seen that Cybertruck and got to thinking. He wasn't gon' pass up the chance to smash. He couldn't wait. Her big ass was wobbling as she sashayed on out the door, giving Hideous an eye full of a nice, big ass.

8:35 p.m.

After Hideous got out of the shower, he quickly threw on a fresh new fit from 28/28 Studios and some new Jays. All he could think about was Ms. Parker and how her ass jiggled up down with every step. He hurried out the door and went straight to Ms. Parker's crib. She moved back a few month's back.

He knocked on the door. It was snatched open with a gun pointed at his face. Standing there was Ms. Parker's only son Shoota Face.

"Who the fuck is you?" he asked in a threatening tone. He stared Hideous up and down.

Shoota Face was Ms. Parker's older, forgotten son. He had just come home from doing a bid down south. He was a scrawny nigga with jet black skin and a lanky, muscular build. Just like Hideous he also was a ruthless human being that would punch you in your shit at any given moment. He picked up the name Shoota Face because of the scar he had on his face. It looked like a bullet wound.

"He's here for mama." A petite, light skinned female appeared next to her brother.

"What?" Shoota Face asked, staring Hideous up and down even harder, but Hideous was unmoved by his intimidation. The notorious stories he had heard about the infamous Shoota Face didn't intimidate him one bit. He was just as relentless as he was, or even more.

Hideous stared him down even harder.

Sarah felt the tension between both men and decided to step in. "Boy, I don't know. I think Mama wanted to talk to him about something that happened the other day over here dealing with them bank robbers."

"Yeah, okay!" he spat before walking off past Hideous. He went out for a walk to clear his head.

"You got to excuse my brother— he ain't got it all in the head, but come in." Sarah turned to lead Hideous inside the house.

His eyes got wide as beach balls. Sarah's ass was stupid fat. She had definitely gotten finer over time.

As soon as Hideous entered the house, he immediately saw shit thrown over and clothes all on the living room floor. They shit looked worse than his own crib.

"Bitch! Don't be talking about me with that bitch ass nigga!" Shoota Face barked as he came back into the house.

"Boy, shut the fuck up and clean this muthafucking house!" she shot back.

Hideous just shook his head. "You sassy and shit now."

"No, I'm not; I just can't stand his funky ass sometimes, and he only been here a week. He just gets on my fucking nerves. *Ugh*!" She cried out. "But I'm about to go anyway. I got accepted to Texas University."

"Oh yeah? My sister got accepted to Texas Women's College in Denton."

"Oh yeah? What about you? What you gon' do with your life? We're all eighteen now."

"School not for me. I chase money now," he said boastfully.

"I see," she said, staring him up and down. "Let me walk you to my mama's room. Follow me." Sarah could feel Hideous' eyes staring at her perfectly round shaped ass. She swished as hard as she could all the way down the hall with

Hideous behind getting an eye full. She wore some short cheerleader shorts that made her ass cheeks bounce with each step she took. She tapped on her mama's bedroom door. "Mama, Reuben out here."

"Okay, I'll be out in a minute."

"I got to get back packing for college. I'll see you later." Before she left, she looked Hideous up and down one more time, then gave him a big ass hug.

Hideous watched as she walked away down the hall. before hearing Ms. Parker's voice.

"Come in Reuben," she said in a seductive voice.

He entered the master bedroom but didn't see any sign of Ms. Parker.

"I'm in the bathroom; I'll be out in a minute. Make yourself comfortable."

"Bet." He sat on the edge of the bed and heard the shower water stop running.

The bathroom door swung open like legs and out came Ms. Parker with nothing on her wet, naked body. Hideous was speechless as he stared at Ms. Parker's flawless body. She looked just like the IG model Bunz4Eva.

"Are you okay, honey?" she asked, spreading apart her pussy lips. "You act like you never seen one of these before."

Hideous didn't know what to say.

"You want me to crawl over to you, daddy?" Ms. Parker would do just about anything for money, and Hideous had plenty of it. He tried to keep it a secret, but the streets talked, and Ms. Parker was actually the only person that witnessed him running away with two duffle bags.

He nodded. His eyes couldn't believe Ms. Parker's big booty ass was on all fours, crawling to him. He leaned against the wall, holding his dick. "Come to me!" he demanded, and Ms. Parker crawled over to him on her hands and knees. Her big ass titties were swinging every which way. "That's a good bitch!" he spat, then walked behind her and smacked her hard on the left ass cheek. He walked back in front of her and looked at her like she was the Mona Lisa.

9:45 p.m.

When Crazy Red pulled up in front of Scream's T. Jones' house he was relieved not to see any sign of her brother. He pulled out his iPhone and texted Scream. He hasn't had time to fuck her since the money was pouring in like a rain flood. Hideous and him were making serious paper, selling all of them pounds around the city to big named hustlers.

Crazy Red: I'm outside you know what it is. And don't forget to delete these messages.

Scream: Whatever!

Crazy Red: Now!

Scream: Ugh, I'm coming. I need to put something on.

Crazy Red: Oh yeah, what you got on?

Scream: Nigga, just a shirt.

Crazy Red: Come like that.

A moment later, when Scream got in Crazy Red's Maserati, he was sitting completely naked I the backseat.

"Hurry up and let's get this over with. I don't know where my brother is."

"He probably with a bitch or sum. I'm not about to sit right here though. I'm 'bout to move just in case he come back to the crib," he said climbing up front. He drove around the block in front of a vacant house and cut the engine. He climbed back in the back with Scream.

Back in Ms. Parker's Bedroom

Hideous swung his dick in Ms. Parker's face. She stretched out her tongue and licked the head of his dick.

"You want this dick in yo' mouth? Huh bitch?"

She nodded her head up and down like a naughty teenage girl. She slowly eased his dick inside of her mouth and started to suck.

"Hold up. Stick yo' tongue out and don't touch me. Let me fuck yo' mouth!"

She did as she was told. She placed her hands on top of her thighs and opened her mouth wide. She stuck her tongue out and let him deep throat her tonsils.

He grabbed the side of her head and shoved his dick inside her mouth as far as it could go. "Open a little wider."

She obeyed. He began fucking her face in. He was pumping in her mouth so fast and hard she gagged and almost threw up on his Jays. He looked down at her. Her eyes were staring up into his. His dick was going in and out of her mouth with speed. He had to admit she was going hard.

When Ms. Parker stood up from her knees, her ass jiggled all over the place; so did her tits. She was gon' reverse cowgirl his young ass, but decided not to, so she turned to face him. She wanted to see his facial expression. She straddled his lap and lifted her big ass up and came down on him hard and quick, giving him no time to prepare himself. She went to work jumping up and down on his nine-inch dick.

Meanwhile, Crazy Red had Scream's legs in the air. He grabbed her by her tiny waist and shoved his dick in her so hard she thought she felt a tear drop.

Crazy Red was going in. He was going faster and faster. He was punishing her good pussy. He fucked her hard and long until he heard her gasp for air. He slid his dick out, leaving just the head in. He was long dicking her with long strokes. Her body started to shake uncontrollably.

She hated her body for turning on her like it did. She had promised herself not to like any of it while he had his way with her body, but she couldn't control the powerful orgasms that were building inside her.

Hideous' hands were palmed tight on Ms. Parker's jiggly ass as he tried his hardest to keep up with the older and much more experienced woman.

"*Harder! Harder! Harder!*" she shouted.

Ms. Parker's legs were spread, her back was bent over the table, and her hair was wrapped around Hideous' wrist as he delivered her with hard strokes. He was trying to knock her back out.

WHAM! WHAM! WHAM!

Ms. Parker's dirty Sprite that was in a red plastic cup, rattled on top of the table. He kept slamming in her.

WHAM! WHAM! Until it finally fell onto the floor.

"Fuck this pussy, nigga," she spat, looking over her shoulder deep into Hideous' eyes. He continued to slam into her for all he was worth.

WHAM! WHAM! WHAM!

She had to admit he did his best shit, but it was her turn now. She pushed him back on the bed and placed a thumb over the tip of his dick to keep it in place as she eased down. This time her back was toward him. She lifted her two hefty ass cheek and began to bounce up and down like a mad woman.

CLAP! CLAP! CLAP!

She sucked in her breath and continued to give Hideous a ride he will never forget.

"Grrrrr!" Hideous growled.

CLAP! CLAP! CLAP! CLAP! CLAP! CLAP!

Mr. Parker jumped off the dick when she felt him about to bust.

"*Ahhh shit*!" He skeeted straight in the air and he roared like a beast.

10:45 p.m.

Hideous walked quietly out of Ms. Parker's crib. He couldn't believe what had just occurred. He replayed Ms. Parker's ass smacking back on him over and over.

As he was walking toward his T. Jones' crib, he saw Crazy Red's Maserati parked in front of a vacant house.

"The fuck he is doing over here?" Hideous said to himself. He walked over to Crazy Red's car. When he approached the car, the first thing he heard was loud moaning coming from the backseat. He crept up along the side of the SUV and peeped inside. What he saw had him seeing red. Crazy Red had his sister's legs up over his shoulders, fucking her brains out.

He could hear his heart thumping as he opened his car door and pulled out his Uzi machine gun with the dick hanging.

"This nigga got me fucked up!" he spat, proceeding across the street with the Uzi in his muthafuckin' hand. Only thing Hideous was focused on was catching a free body. His heart threatened to leap out his chest as he got closer to Crazy Red's car.

"What this ugly ass nigga on?" Shoota Face said as he stood against the darkness of the wall of the vacant house, where he had just fucked a crack head. He was now on his way back to his T. Jones' crib until he seen a dark figure holding a gun walking in his direction. He witnessed the horror that unfolded.

Hideous pointed the machine gun at Crazy Red's car and yelled, "Get the fuck out the car, Rachel!" It sounded as if he was talking in slow motion for a second.

Scream looked over at Crazy Red. He looked terrified. She smiled at the thought of him dying.

As soon as her feet touched the pavement, Hideous let the machine gun bark.

BUDDABUDDA! BUDDABUDDA!

"What the fuck!" Shoota Face couldn't believe what he was witnessing. The shooting went on for a couple of seconds.

Hideous walked away like nothing had happened with smoke coming out his toolie.

Scream, on the other hand, glanced inside Crazy Red's shot up car. He was stretched out with a shitload of bullets bloody bullet holes. He was definitely going to have a closed casket.

CHAPTER 8

Crime Scene Investigation

"Can somebody cover his body, for God's sakes!" Detective Mark D. Anthony barked.

Mark D. Anthony had been with Dallas Homicide for fourteen years, and even with everything he'd seen, this one hit different.

"Whoever did this had a vendetta toward that young man," Detective Ward said, staring at Crazy Red's lifeless body as they lifted him onto the gurney.

Shoota Face stood silent while Crackhead Neka paced, tears streaking her face.

"We gotta tell the authorities what we saw. *Ms. Cash's son shot Chris*," she said. Shoota Face didn't respond, just watched her wear a groove in the floor.

After the shooting, he'd slipped back in the vacant with Neka's cracked-out self. She had him twisted if she thought he was about to go ratting.

"Did you hear what I said?" she pressed. "We have to—"

"*Bitch,* I'm not no rat," he snapped, peeking through the blinds at the detectives getting back in their Crown Vic. His blood heated as anger crawled up his spine.

"Well, what we supposed to do? We can't just sit and do nothing."

Shoota Face ignored her, watching the last investigators pack up and leave. When the street finally cleared, he looked back at Neka still pacing. Her ass bounced under that dingy muscle shirt, and he hated that he noticed it—fine or not, she was trouble.

He turned to leave when she asked, “Where you going?”

“Damn, bitch, to piss. You need to sign off on that too?” he muttered, mean-mugging her before he stepped outside.

Behind the house, he grabbed a heavy rock off the ground. When he eased back in, she didn’t even notice him at first. She turned around—

Too late.

The rock cracked against her forehead. Blood spilled, and she crumpled. She threw her arms up, trying to protect herself, but he kept swinging until she stopped moving. When he stepped back, she was gone. Unrecognizable.

He dropped the rock beside her and stepped around the spreading pool on the floor.

A few days later…

Hideous was stretched out on his king-size bed, watching one of his favorite movies on his iPad. Three days since Crazy Red died—and three days since *he* killed his best friend.

Red was like a brother. And yeah, Hideous loved him, but loyalty was loyalty. Scream had shown him the texts, told him everything that happened. Maybe she was messy for how she handled it, but she wasn’t lying.

He turned the volume up at his favorite part—the scene where Tony walked in and found Manny with Gina.

Boom.

Just like that, Tony pulled the trigger. Just like Hideous had pulled his. Loyalty violated was loyalty buried.

He’d helped Crazy Red’s baby mama with funeral arrangements the other day, and not one drop of remorse touched him.

“I can’t believe he’s dead, Reuben,” Val cried over the phone.

“Me either, ma. But I promise I’ma find who did this.”

"You promise? Say you promise, Reuben."

"I promise I'ma find the muthafucka and handle it myself."

"Thank you."

"I'ma come bring you the rest of Red's money later," he added. *And maybe get something out of it,* he thought, jaw tight.

"The Lord knows I need it for me and Chris Jr.," she sniffed.

After he hung up, he sat on the edge of the bed, rolled a blunt, and sparked it. Halfway through, his phone buzzed—Facebook message.

Lil_Sarah_TooThrowed_Savage: *So you really calling yourself Hideous? I added you, go accept it right now.*

Hideous_makeitrainCash: *I just did. What you on?*

Lil_Sarah: *Nothing. You heard about Crackhead Neka?*

Hideous: *Naw, what happened?*

Lil_Sarah: *Turn on the news. Somebody killed her in Mr. Anthony's old house. Same place Chris died. They say it was drug-related.*

Hideous: *Damn. I'm still messed up about my nigga.*

Lil_Sarah: *Aww, come keep me company. My brother gone and my mama somewhere taking somebody's husband money lol.*

Hideous: *I'm on the way.*

He stood up, already dressed head to toe in his usual drip.

When he started out the front door, his mama's voice cut through the room. She was laid out on the couch.

"I know yo dumb ass ain't 'bout to walk out that door. The whole block crawling with police."

"What?" he asked, stomach flipping.

"They found Crackhead Neka in that old Anthony house. Before they found her, the whole street was funky. Smelled like something big died on Messa Circle."

"It was that bad?" Hideous chuckled.

"Chile, *yeah*," she grimaced.

Hearing it out loud shook him more than he expected. Neka got taken out damn near where he handled Crazy Red.

That meant somebody else out there was moving.

"Whoever the pussy is gon' die. There better not be no witnesses," Hideous muttered, snatching up his Uzi.

CHAPTER 9

No Witnesses

Shoota Face been laying low ever since he killed Crack Head Neka a week ago. The detectives been knocking from door to door for the last couple of days for any eyewitnesses to the double murders but came up short. No one was talking.

Word on the streets was that a family across the street witnessed the whole ordeal; from beginning to end, but didn't catch the killer's face.

But that still didn't do too well with Shoota Face.

"I'm gon' to have to pay them a visit!" Shoota Face spat.

3:19 p.m.

Caprice pulled down her dress over her juicy ass for the umpteenth time. She wore a tight Prada dress with no panties on underneath. Hideous was sitting on of the hood of his Cybertruck. He eyeballed her as she sashayed toward him.

"Damn, bae, how do you expect me to get in that?" She said, pointing at the Telsa.

"Girl, you betta hop in," he spat, hopping off the hood.

"Boy, everybody and their mama gon' see I'm not wearing any panties," she hissed as she climbed in the big whip. As she predicted, her small dress hiked over her fat ass, giving whoever was out there an eye full. Seeing her not wearing any panties, Hideous beamed with excitement.

She ran her hands over the seats, looking around, amazed at the two televisions he had installed. “Bae, this she lit!” she said, still looking around his ride.

Hideous glanced over and saw her thick thighs. His dick instantly grew an extra inch inside his 28/28 joggers. She peeped him checking her out of her peripheral vision, so she purposely crossed her thick red legs; the hem of her tight dress quickly sliding up far enough that her pretty bald pussy was peeking.

Hideous had to hold his composure and pray that his dick didn’t pop out at full salute. But before he had time to erase the thought, he felt Caprice’s hands pulling down his pants.

Twenty minutes later, Hideous was flying down 67 South just leaving Big T Plaza and now was heading toward Red Bird Mall. The two fifteens in the Cybertruck had the entire truck shaking with Headhuncho Amir’s new hit *Motivate the City*. He had the video playing on both TVs.

He looked down as Caprice covered half his dick with her mouth. “Hmmm… keep sucking that fat dick.”

GAK! GAK! GAK!

She’d been sucking his dick non-stop for a hot lil minute now. Her mouth started to hurt.

“Fuck, that feels good!” He grabbed the back of her head. “Pull those sexy tits out.” He looked down for a second when all he heard was somebody blowing their horn.

BEEP! BEEP!

He almost hit the side of a black Porsche 911. His Telsa was inches away from slamming into it, until the driver caught a glimpse and blew his horn.

“Damn, my nigga! You gone make a nigga wreck!” The yella nigga with long dreads shouted.

“Nigga, fuck you!” Hideous threw him the fuck you finger and displaying his Uzi machine gun he had tucked underneath the seat.

“Yeah, bitch made ass nigga!” Caprice yelled with a mouth full of spit on the side of her chin. She also pointed the middle finger at the yella nigga. She was doing shit she didn't used to do. She stared at him as if she was looking at him for the very first time. She had to admit she felt safe with him. She could be her goofy self. She knew he'd been torn up about his best friend's death. She almost forgot about his funeral. "Crazy Red's funeral today, right?"

"Yeah, that's why I'm looking for something to wear. But Big T didn't have shit."

"Where it's gonna be held at?"

"Golden Gate Funeral Home."

Just when Hideous was about to exit Camp Wisdom, his iPhone began to ring. He stared at the screen. His eyes lit up. It was Sarah.

"Sarah!" he quickly pushed the talk button. "What I owe to this unpleasant surprise?"

"Where you at? I know who witnessed Crazy Red's murder. The same person might be responsible for killing Crack Head Neka. Or seen it too. Get over here fast!" Sarah said quickly.

The words hit Hideous like a ton of bricks. Somebody had witnessed him killing his best friend, and he had to do something about it. The witness had to die, and he didn't care who it was. He quickly busted a U-turn, heading back toward the Nawf.

"Daddy, is everything okay?" Caprice asked, looking concerned.

"It's going to be. Trust me," he replied, sitting his Uzi on his lap.

4:52p.m.

Thirty minutes later, he dropped Caprice off at her T. Jones' crib. He drove 75 miles-per-hour down Harry Hines. He made a quick right on Record Crossing. He cut the music down because his two fifteens sounded like King Kong and Godzilla was trapped in the Cybertruck getting it on.

5:00p.m.

"My son didn't see shit! I swear!" Ed Green said with both hands in the air.

On the left of Ed Green sat his terrified wife. She shook her head from side to side. Her husband had warned her to keep her mouth shut about what their nine-year-old son, who was sitting next to her with his head dropped down staring at his fidgeting hands, had witnessed. The boy was scared shitless. And he should. Standing in front of them was Shoota Face holding a loaded gun.

"Shut the fuck up!" WHAM! Shoota Face hit Ed Green across the face with the butt of the gun so hard blood gushed instantly.

He doubled over in severe pain. "*Got dammit*!" Ed Green roared.

"Now, I'm gon' ask you again, lil' man. What did you tell the cops?" Shoota Face pointed the gun at the little boy's head.

Sweat ran down the boy's face, and tears began to well in his eyes.

"Please, sir, my son didn't see anything. I did," the woman lied.

Shoota Face was fed up and placed the barrel of the gun to the bitch's forehead and blew her lying thoughts out the back of her skull. The father got it too.

The young boy watched as both of his parents' brains splattered in two different directions. Shoota Face stepped back and looked at the young boy who had just peed on himself. He shook his head in disgust. He was just about to send the young boy where he had just sent his parents when a black Cybertruck pulled up in front of the Green's yard.

"What the fuck he wants?" Shoota Face mumbled. "Get yo' nasty ass up!" He quickly snatched the boy from the bloody sofa.

5:07p.m.

Hideous cautiously walked up on the front porch with his Uzi at his side. He looked around to make sure the coast was clear. The only people that could be seen were a bunch of young boys playing tackle football.

When he pressed his ear against the door, to his surprise the door opened.

"The fuck?" Hideous eased into the house with his Uzi clutched tight like a bad kid at the Fair.

As he quietly walked further into the house he stopped. There was so much blood all over the floor and furniture. To his surprise there were two dead bodies slumped on the floor.

"What you doing here, nigga? I had the shit under control," a raspy voice came from the far-left side of the living room.

Hideous was so fucked up by the two dead bodies, he didn't even see Shoota Face standing there with a frightened young boy standing in front of him. He had his gun pressed to the side of the boy's tiny head.

Hideous mugged the shit outta Shoota Face. *Why was he there cleaning up his mess, unless Sarah couldn't hold water?* At first, he thought his eyes were playing tricks on him, but they weren't. Shoota Face was standing there in the flesh with a young boy held at gun point.

"Why is you here? This don't concern you." Hideous spat, not putting together the pieces. Then it finally hit him. "You the one who killed Crack Head Neka! But why?"

An evil smirk crept onto Shoota Face's face. "The bitch wanted me to snitch on you for what we saw you do to Crazy Red. But I ain't no damn snitch!" he spat. "And how I see it, you and I are halfway alike."

"And what make you think that?"

"Because when I look into yo' eyes, I see nothing."

BOOM! BOOM!

Just like Hideous, Shoota Face also had his demons. Hideous looked at the child that now lay lifeless on the floor with two nickel size holes in the side of his head. His blood went everywhere, making the already bloody living room even bloodier. His blood splattered all over Hideous' all-white forces

"Damn, my nigga! Why you kill the lil nigga?" Hideous asked as he moved toward the front door.

"Hold up, I got a better idea." Shoota Face said. He turned and walked toward the kitchen. He came back with a butcher knife.

"Man, what the fuck you gon' do with that?"

CHAPTER 10

The Funeral

"It's bad, sir. Somebody even cut the young boy's eyes out," the uniformed officer said.

Detective Mark D. Anthony shut his eyes, trying to block the image forming in his mind. Two days ago, he'd spoken to that boy's mama. Now the whole family was gone—slaughtered. Eyes missing. Blood everywhere.

When he stepped inside the house, it hit him hard. Three bodies. Three puddles of blood. And the nine-year-old boy lying there with two bullet holes in his head.

"Who would do this to a kid?" he growled, voice tight. He wiped a tear before it could fall. In all his years with homicide, he'd never cried on a scene. But this one… this one cut into him.

Eight years earlier…

Patrol cars lined his parents' street. Mark barely got the car stopped before he ran.

"Not my fath—"He choked on the words.

His father lay in dried blood that turned the grass dark. His mother stood above him, her white church dress stained red. She must've held him after he fell.

Mark froze, eyes burning. He hadn't seen that image in years, but standing over this new crime scene, it punched the breath from his lungs. His father's case had gone cold eight years ago, but the vow he made never did.

Find the killer.And when he found him, put him down.

"You sure you want this case?" Detective Hill asked softly. "Being back in your old neighborhood… this house… it might bring up things you don't want to deal with."

"I'm good," he said, pulling her close by the waist.

She looked up into his eyes. She knew he wasn't good. His fiancée could always see past the mask. She'd loved him long before she'd ever been his partner, and he respected her concern.

But he wasn't letting this one go.

The murder of Chris Thomas came across his desk with a familiar address—the same house his parents once owned—and Mark ran to it.

Saturday Morning

9:45 a.m.

Crazy Red's funeral was packed. Folks crying everywhere, the whole place heavy with grief. Closed casket, just like Hideous knew it would be.

A blown-up picture of him and Crazy Red sat in front of the gold casket. Hideous had to admit—Crazy Red's baby mama put him away nice.

Lady Love, Red's mama, sat in the front. She never liked Hideous much, but losing her only child had her slumped forward, broken. Val sat beside her with Chris Jr. in her lap—one year old, clapping, smiling, playing, not knowing his daddy was never coming home.

Hideous sat right behind them, staring at the picture of him and Red shoulder to shoulder. He felt nothing. No guilt. No weight.

Scream leaned into him, sobbing, snotting on his shoulder. He wanted to push her off him. This whole mess was her fault, and everybody grieving. That was on her too. When she looked up and smiled like she was doing the perfect grieving act, he had to admit the girl could win an award for faking.

After the service, Hideous slipped to the back of the funeral home, ready to get back to the money.

A few feet away, Val finished talking to one of Red's cousins. When she spotted Hideous, she walked over, arms opening before she even reached him. She collapsed onto his chest, crying hard.

"I can't believe he's gone, Reuben. Who did this to him? Please… tell me."

"I don't know," he lied. "I wish I did."

"Promise me you'll kill the one who did it. Promise me, Reuben."

"I promise."

"Thank you. You always been there for us. If it wasn't for you, none of this—none of the funeral—would've happened."

"You know I got y'all. Whatever you need, just say it."

She kissed his cheek, then walked away. Hideous watched her hips move under that pencil skirt. The way she walked could stop traffic. His thoughts drifted places they shouldn't—until a thick white woman walked through the door.

"*Bitch, I know you didn't show your face at my husband's funeral!*" Val snapped at her.

"*I can bring my daughter to see her daddy one last time!* You don't have no say," the blonde woman shot back, holding a pretty mixed baby on her hip.

"*Fuck you and your daughter, bitch!*"

"*Bitch, fuck you and your ugly son, hoe!*"

Val charged. Before anybody could react, punches flew. The blonde screamed about her baby, and an older Black woman snatched the child out her arms.

"Chile, give me that baby. I don't know why y'all actin' a fool at this boy's funeral!"

The women went at it like wrestlers—wild swings, clothes slipping, hair flying. The funeral director and two men pulled them apart.

"Bitch, you going to jail for hitting my daughter!" the blonde yelled as she got dragged away.

"Bitch, fuck that ugly baby, hoe!"

Hideous rushed in and grabbed Val from the pastor and the men holding her back.

He pulled her toward the exit.

"Girl, pull your skirt down. You showing the whole room everything." Her skirt was damn near at her waist. "Who was that? I didn't know Red had a daughter. I thought Chris Jr. was the only kid."

"I did too. Until I found out he cheated on me around the time I got pregnant."

"Damn. That's messed up."

"It's whatever." She yanked her skirt back into place. Tattoos covered her whole backside—stars, butterflies, everything. Hideous couldn't help staring.

"This whole thing is crazy. My baby's father dead, and that bitch ruined his funeral," she said, eyes watering again.

"It's gon' be alright. I'm gon' avenge my nigga's death. I promise." He wrapped his arms around her. "You hear me? I promise."

Val nodded and cried into his chest, thinking, *what a funeral.*

CHAPTER 11

Massacre

Hideous drove his new BMW i8 through the sunny side of South Dallas. He was stacking more paper with Shoota Face than he ever did with Crazy Red. He and Shoota Face had become real tight. He felt kind of bad. He was still fucking the shit out of his mama, but that will be another issue he'll have to deal with when that day came. But for now, he was living life, making close to 10 racks a week.

Shoota Face had implied that they needed to sell something heavier than weed. He promised that they would make a lot more money which they did once Hideous told his connect he wanted to sell some White Bitch. So, his plugged introduced him to an opioid drug that was killing people and giving niggas life in prison. But he didn't give a fuck. Greed done took over his mental. He wasn't scared to supply the world with Fentanyl.

Being the only nigga in the city with some cartel shit, Hideous quickly flipped what he was making selling pounds of Za. Now he had that White Girl, and everybody and their mama wanted to fuck her.

He rode with his Uzi machine gun on his lap as usual. Not because he was in the roughest part of the city and the murder rate was at its highest in the South, but he rode with two kilos. Each slut was priced at 26 racks a piece.

In The Trap

“Give me another hit!” the hood rat spat with attitude. She was under the table on all fours between Shoota Face’s legs. She had just gotten done sucking up all his babies like a Whirlwind vacuum cleaner.

“Hold up, bitch, you gone fuck up my concentration!” he barked stuffing small baggies with a gram of weed.

“Uggghhh!” she hissed.

“Shut up and put that dick back in yo’ mouth!” He didn’t have to wait for long. He felt her wet, sloppy tongue wrap back around his dick.

Brittney sucked on it like she was trying to get to the center of a Tootsie Roll pop.

“Damn! Bitch!” he nodded his head back in pleasure while Brittney’s mouth went to work.

As soon as Hideous pulled up to the spot, he saw a lot of people hanging around— mostly crackheads pacing back and forth like zombies, waiting for Shoota Face to open up shop. It looked all too real to Hideous how they were lined up waiting. You would have thought the latest pair of Jays had arrived.

Hideous grabbed the Goyard bag concealing the two bad bitches. He opened the door, which came up like a butterfly wing. He clutched his machine gun and threw the bag over his shoulder. As soon as his red bottom Gucci loafers hit the pavement, a big booty crack head ran up on him.

“Bitch, get back, hoe.” He pointed the Uzi in her face as he looked her up and down.

“I haven’t got my check yet, but I got something you might be interesting in.” She turned with her back facing him and lifted her dingy dress over her chunky ass.

Hideous turned and walked away. She grabbed him by the arm with the strength of a man. He slapped her hand away roughly and barked.

“Bitch, don’t put yo’ dirty ass hands on me!”

“Please, just give me something to get the monkey off my back. I’ll do anything,” she begged.

"Bitch! You better go around the corner with that bullshit. Them niggas in Park Row got some of the same shit."

"Hell naw. Nobody shit get my pussy wetter! Yo' shit on a whole other planet."

Hideous had to laugh at that. He knew the crackhead was telling the truth. Just the other day he heard three people overdosed fuckin' with that shit. He tried to go past the crackhead, but this time she jumped in front of him, clearly shook up by the warning he gave her about ever touching him again.

"Please, I suck yo' dick! And everybody up in there. Please," she begged, dropping to her knees in front of him, reaching for his pants.

Hideous looked over and saw a lot of people that weren't looking to shoot up out and about on that pretty sunny day. That's the only reason the crackhead kept her life, but that still didn't save her from getting kneed in the face.

WHAM! The crackhead fell over, holding her now bloody nose. Hideous stepped over her and quickly jogged up the steps. He walked around back and pulled open the screen door and stepped inside.

The first thing that greeted him was Brittney's round ass and her hairy pussy. She was under the table going in on Shoota Face's dick. Shoota Face smiled and put a finger up to his lips, indicating Hideous to be quiet. Hideous walked over and sat the Goyard bag on the table. He grabbed the pistol grip 12 gauge that laid peacefully on the table and walked to the living room.

For a junkie, Brittney's two-bedroom house was spotless and decked out with top of the art and electronics. "I bet a booster paid off," Hideous said to himself as he sat on the sectional part of the black leather sofa.

Other than the slurping sounds coming from the kitchen, the trap was dead silent. Hideous turned on the 75-inch flat screen and turned to ESPN. He was trying to catch the NFL DRAFT preview to see who the Dallas Cowboys were going to pick up in the first round when he jumped to a loud noise from the kitchen.

"Bitch, get the fuck off me!"

Hideous heard a loud smack.

SLAP!

A second later, Shoota Face walked in the living room. He had a stack of money in one hand and a half a zip of weed in the other.

"You ready to turn the fuck up tonight, baby boy?" All he wore was some jays and a pair of Versace briefs.

Hideous could tell he was coked up. "Damn, fam, you alright?" Hideous asked.

"Man, I didn't ask you that. I said is you ready to turn the fuck up!"

"Yeah, I'm ready."

"We gon' turn up for real." Shoota Face was sitting there with glazed eyes.

"Hell naw! You got to get the fuck up outta hur. You done bust my lip, bitch ass nigga!" a naked Brittney growled as she walked over and got in front of the 75-inch. "Get the fuck out. You, yo' partner, and drugs!" she shouted, folding her arms over her bare chest.

"Bitch, you gone embarrass me like that in front of my business partner? Huh, bitch?"

Hideous looked into Shoota Face's cold eyes and saw it all too well. He had the eyes of a killer. Before Hideous could stop him, the damage was already done.

Shoota Face leaped up off the couch, grabbing the pistol-grip shotgun that sat in Hideous' lap. He took aim at the crackhead and pulled the trigger. A loud roar boomed through the house, bouncing off the walls. The sound thudded through Hideous' skull, rattling his brain.

The shot tore through the crackhead's torso. Her chest exploded outward in all directions. Blood tainted the air crimson. She dropped backwards onto the floor dead, her insides leaking from her shredded chest.

Hideous sat there unmoved by the gruesome scene that unfolded in front of his own two eyes. He was too numb to pain to care.

Shoota Face walked back over to the couch and sat next to Hideous. He resumed their conversation like nothing had just taken place.

"Say, fam, we gone turn up for real tonight. But on some real shit, we got to get our shit and get the fuck up outta here. I know them crack heads heard all that shooting!" Shoota face said, "But I do got an idea."

"Yeah, what's that?"

"Go get the guns out from under the bed. We got to kill everybody."

A couple of minutes later, Shoota Face invited in the remaining crack heads that were still out in the front of the trap. The ones that were smart took off once they heard the gun shots go off.

Hideous sat and stared at the six crackheads with a disgusting look written all over his face. Especially the big booty crackhead he kicked earlier that day. All six of them were on that shit bad— tying ropes around their arms, shooting up, while a dead bitch laid in a pool of her own blood right in front of them.

Blood was splattered all over the walls and floor, but they didn't know more blood was going to be shed.

Laughing, one of the crackheads slipped behind the big booty one, rubbing his crotch all over her ass. She looked to be struggling, trying to pull away. But she was high as hell.

The crackhead began to squeeze her tits, kneading them through the thin material of her dress. He then hooked his fingers over the top of the material and yanked it down, tearing it with ease, exposing the crackhead tits to the cool night air.

"Oh, no! Look at what we have here," another crackhead said, squeezing her tits, twisting her nipples between his thumb and forefinger.

Both crackheads were laughing hysterically.

"Make her suck yo' dick." Shoota Face said with a wicked smile.

"That's a great idea." Said the one that yanked her dress down. He made her get on her knees. He unzipped his jeans and withdrew his throbbing erection. "You want some of this, youngster?"

All the crackheads were surrounding the big booty crackhead waiting their turn. Shoota Face had eased to the back.

"Fuck naw!" Hideous shot back.

Shoota face walked back into the living room with an evil look on his face, a blunt in his mouth, and an AK-47 in his hands. His expression hardened as he stared at the scene before him. He aimed at the crackheads and ripped them apart.

BUDDABUDDA! BUDDABUDDA!

"Nasty ass niggas!" screamed Shoota Face.

Hideous jumped in the chaos, blasting at the crackhead that tried to flee, hitting him three times in the back. When the bullets stopped. Both men were nowhere to be found. It was seven bodies sprawled out in very bad shape.

Detective Mark Anthony walked into the bloody house and shook his head at the seven dead bodies, two women and the rest men. All of them had been shot more than a dozen times. They were sprawled out on the bloody floor; he stepped up to the first body who was a young black woman. Her chest was no longer intact to her body. She was dismantled.

"Can somebody please come cover her up, please!" he asked as he looked around.

"Her name is Brittney Woods. The house belongs to her. No job, no kids. She been arrested for minor theft charges, nothing too major," the FBI Agent said. "It looks like a drug deal gone terribly bad."

"And who the hell is you? And where is my partner?"

"I'm FBI agent Lucy Ross. The FBI will be conducting this case now. It's been brought to my attention that drugs were involved. We believe the Chinese cartel put a hit out on this specific location for a reason," she said with her pen and notepad in her hand.

"Um, the Chinese Cartel? Not El Chapo, right? Are you fucking serious? This is my case. A bunch of low life scum of the world did this; not no fucking cartel."

"Well, excuse me, but if you would like to follow me, I will show you evidence that gives me solid proof that this was the work of the Red Dragon Cartel." FBI agent Lucy Ross led him down the hall to the bedroom and showed him a couple of stamped logos in Chinese letters on top of some wrinkled up plastic. "See those? That's the initials of the Red Dragon Cartel. A highly dangerous organization in the northern region. Are you familiar with the name Suwoo Chan?"

"Of course not. Who the hell is that?" Detective Anthony asked.

"The most feared man in China, and we believe he's transporting kilos of pure cocaine into the country. I have been investigating him for nearly two years, and I really think he was responsible for this massacre crime."

"You got to give me more evidence than that."

"I don't have to give you shit. This is my case now. You can get the fuck out."

CHAPTER 12

Gentlemen's Club

Monday 11:45

It's been two days since the massacre, and Shoota Face could give two fucks about it. Every time they played the tragic murders on the news he would quickly change the channel.

The day had finally come for him and Hideous to turn up. The night they were supposed to turn up ended up being tragic, so they decided Money Wars Monday at DG's would be a perfect place to celebrate the numbers that were flooding their pockets, and Shoota Face couldn't wait any longer. He had never made so much money in his entire life.

Shoota Face moved around his new trap arranging guns under the expensive furniture for safe keeping, just in case a stick-up kid decided to be stupid.

He walked over and grabbed a box full of money and pulled out a scale and placed it on the glass coffee table in front of him. He sat down on the white leather sofa and reached for the Goyard bag Hideous gave him the night of the shooting.

Not having time to explore the bag, he opened it and was extremely satisfied with the contents.

"Damn, these some sexy ass white bitches," he stated out loud as he reached and pulled out the two kilos. "Yeah, I'm gon' name you two bitches Mary Kate and Ashley," he said caressing each of like a mother would her newborn baby.

The sound of the doorbell caused Shoota Face to jump. He quickly rushed to one of his guns hidden under one of the furniture pieces. He gripped a chrome, his favorite Glock, and moved over to check the 42-inch monitor. Once he saw who it was, he let out a sigh of relief.

"What it do, nigga?" Hideous asked as he walked over and sat on the sofa.

"Is you ready for tonight?"

"Hell yeah, I'm ready." He pulled out a brick of money from his 2828 jeans and flashed it.

"I see ya, baby boy."

"Say, I heard DG's gon' be turned up. It's all on the Gram." Hideous said.

"Well, we gone have to see about that. Hold up, let me go get dressed. Here. Drank on this until I'm finished." Shoota Face handed him a bottle of Don Julio.

"Damn! You trying to get a nigga fucked up tonight." Hideous spat.

A few minutes later, Shoota Face entered the living room clean as hell. He wore a white 2828 graphic tee. "You ready nigga?" he asked as his three bussdown Cubans swung back and forth. As he walked out the door he grabbed his Glock.

"Nigga, you showing out," Hideous said as they both hopped in his BMW i8 dollar.

Club DG's
1:00a.m.

"Damn, how many people are inside?" Hideous said as they pulled up on the side of DG's. The line was wrapped around the building. Mostly with hoes with fat asses and in small dresses.

"Damn! Look at that bitch right there," said Shoota Face from the passenger seat. He was pointing at a thick, big booty red bone wearing half to nothing. Her small Gucci dress wasn't protecting her fat ass at all. Every time she pulled her dress down, her fat ass would lift it back up.

Hideous hopped out of his whip with his hand wrapped around his gun. He tucked it inside his waistband as he moved toward the front of the club. He looked over his shoulder and saw Shoota Face pulling out his big iPhone 17, getting big red's number.

Once inside the packed strip club, big asses bounced all around the club. Strippers from all over the city were in the building tonight, shaking ass and big, naked titties.

When Hideous looked to his side, Shoota Face was scrolling through his phone. "Who that bitch was?" Hideous asked.

"A lil freak hoe. She says she work here and she gon' turn up for me. Her name was Susie."

"Susie? That name sounds familiar. Real shit."

"Man, say hold up. Is that Erica Banks and Just Britteny over there kissing?" Shoota Face asked, pointing in the direction by the bar.

"It look like it," Hideous replied, looking at the two kissing and giggling amongst each other.

"Them two is the baddest bitches in the game in Texas right now. See Erica with the black and gold body suit? She got to have my kids. I swear I'll drank her bath water. Real talk."

Hideous had to admit they were the bad, but the club was packed with bad bitches.

1:20a.m.

Hideous and Shoota Face sat in the VIP room. Hideous had his hands folded on top of the table where he had money stacked up like he just robbed a Brinks truck. He looked over and saw Shoota Face poppin' one of the blue bands containing one-dollar bills. He threw the whole thing in the air, then popped another and did the same exact shit. After a short while, it was flooding nothing but dead presidents in the VIP area.

"Damn, daddy, let me make some of that money," the big booty stripper spat, reaching toward the money that sat on the table.

Hideous instantly slapped her hands aside and said, "You got to earn that money, lil' mama."

"Hell yeah, you do," Shoota Face agreed as he cuffed her ass with two hands and squeezed them hoes.

Bunz 4ever took one look at Hideous and could tell he was getting munyun, and plenty of it. He was fly as hell wearing a 2828 fit. On top of that, his bussdown Cuban link with the big medallion piece swinging on his neck that read *Hideous* looked like a Christmas tree dripped. It was lighting up that whole area. Bunz immediately started shaking her ass in Hideous' face, making that big ass jump one cheek at a time.

Left, right, left, right, her cheeks jumped on her and bounced like a basketball. Shoota Face smacked one, then the other. Her ass moved like an earthquake had just hit the building.

Bunz was so focused on the stacks of money that were piled high on top of the round table that she didn't hear the DJ call her name for the umpteenth time. She just continued to bounce her massive ass.

"Bunz! It's time for us to perform. You know if we're late it's gonna come out the money we made tonight, girl," Butt-Butt said with her hands on her small waist as she rolled her neck.

"Bitch, hold the fuck up. I can cover whatever. These niggas lit over here. Look at all the money I done made," said Bunz, pointing at the floor where money was piled high above her ankles. Bunz picked a handful of money up and threw it in the air while she continued to make her ass clap. "Yeah, bitch, I'm getting money over hur!" she yelled while she threw nothing but ass from side to side.

"Yeah, come make some money over here with us. We not like these other niggas, love. We gon' show love," Hideous informed, staring at the way Bunz's cheeks did a fool. Her huge ass was literally in a hood to hood fight the way it clapped against each other.

"We can pay whatever," Shoota Face confirmed, looking down at the fat blunt he was rolling up.

"Boy, I hear ya!" she said with some attitude.

Hideous' eyes traveled down to inspect Butt-Butt's body, because her face was on point. "Damn, get the fuck out of here. That's not all you," Hideous said. The ass and hips on Butt-Butt were unreal.

Butt-Butt didn't reply, she just made that ass clap together with her hands in the air. It made a loud clapping sound. "What you think?"

"Dammmmmnnn!" she heard again but this time from Shoota face. He was done rolling his blunt and looked up in time to see an ass big as hell bouncing up and down.

Hideous still couldn't get over how slim she was, but her ass was enormous.

"Fuck that stage, ma. Stay over here and fuck with my boy. I can see he's feeling you. Don't worry about me; I got mines," said Shoota, Face grabbing a half-naked Bunz and sitting her on his lap.

"Yeah, fuck with me. Fuck that stage." Hideous pulled out a stack of money that was too big to fold.

Butt-Butt's eyes got big. She was fucking with some rich niggas, but she played it cool and said, "Boy, I can't do noting with you. Yo' ass is too damn skinny. All this ass…" She turned to show him what 50 inches of ass look like. "…will suffocate you when I sit on yo' face," she teased.

"Bitch, come make this money." He smiled, showing nothing but platinum.

Butt-Butt stood there for a second, checking him from head to toe. Other than the fact he looked like he been in a very bad fire, he was good with her. Or should she say his paper was good for her. She looked over at Bunz. She was bouncing her big ass up and down on Shoota Face's lap.

1:50a.m.

DG's locker room

Big Booty Susie had just made a little over three racks fuckin' with Cool Money ENT. She put the trash bag full of dead presidents in her locker and stepped out the Cool Money ENT boy shorts that hugged the inside of her ass cheeks like a thong, then she lifted the white and red Cool Money ENT halter top over her head, and she sauntered around the locker room butt ass naked. She knew all the other hoes envied her because she brought in all the money at the end of the day.

Turning to face the full-length mirror, Susie stared at her money maker. All her life she had a grown woman's body. She had hips, big titties, and a humongous ass.

"Damn, my ass is so fat. Yeah, even bigger than them two hoes, Bunz and Butt-Butt," she said as she smiled at what looked back at it. "I'm 'bout to kill these hoes. I'm not done. Everybody dropping out tonight." She bent over, touching her ankles and began to make her ass cheeks clap together. She did her hair and made sure it was on point before leaving the locker room.

"Damn, lil' mama." One broke nigga said and reached out and grabbed an exposed ass cheek.

She wanted to turn around and go off on his broke, dusty ass, but she just kept it moving with all eyes beaming on her fat ass booty. She put a little more swish in her hips, throwing that ass every which way.

"Damn! That shit there don't make no damn sense," she heard from one of the broke niggas. She couldn't do nothing but smile. She had to admit she enjoyed the attention.

She spotted Shoota Face in VIP. After all, he wasn't hard to find with all the bussdowns around his neck and wrist. He had a bad bitch she couldn't stand bouncing ass on his lap. She boldly walked right up to where he was seated, extended her hand and said, "Hey, you remember me?"

"Damn, how can I forget?" He smiled and grabbed her by the hand and swirled her around. Shoota Face had to bite down on his fist. Her ass was as big as two blue berry muffins.

Bunz stopped bouncing her ass and looked up at Susie. "Bitch, can't you see me entertaining him?" Bunz started back bouncing on Shoota Face's lap as if she was a kid bouncing on a trampoline. But seeing Susie still standing there, Bunz smacked her lips and said, "Damn! Bitch, can't you move around?"

Susie smiled. "I think he's a big boy to handle the both of us."

Bunz rolled her eyes and looked over her shoulder at Shoota Face. He had a Kool-Aid smile across his face.

"You know what?" she shot, snatching her bra off the table. "I don't share with competition." Bunz shot up from his lap and marched around where her best friend was grinding up against Hideous' lap.

They both were unaware of the heated argument between the two ladies.

"Let's go!" Bunz barked, slipping back on her bra.

"Why? What happened?" Butt-Butt asked, not wanting to miss out on all the money Hideous was tricking off.

"I'm just ready to go."

Hideous looked over at Shoota Face who had an even larger ass now bouncing in his lap.

Just then Susie looked up and smiled, but her smile quickly faded when she locked eyes with Hideous. "Oh my God!" she whispered as she looked into the eyes that killed her best friend's baby daddy.

"Everything good?" Shoota Face asked when her ass stopped jumping like hydraulics. He reached out and cuffed one. It was soft and juicy and felt like he'd stuck his hand inside two big birthday cakes.

Susie jumped when she felt his hand grip her ass.

"Damn! Is you okay?"

"Yeah, I'm good. You just scared me. But I got to go get ready for the main stage. Hit me up after. I'm leaving with you tonight."

Shoota Face watched as Susie strolled off. He took a long pull on the blunt he was smoking between his lips. He pictured that it was Susie's pussy lips. She had promised him she was going to leave with him once she got off, and he couldn't wait until he could put his lips on her pussy.

Shoota Face's eyes drifted back to the bullshit that played out in front of him. He closed his eyes and counted to five. But that shit didn't work. He looked up at Bunz's gigantic ass waving at him. The neon lights flashed against Bunz and Butt-Butt, literally playing tug-a-war with Hideous' long tongue.

Shoota Face could feel his anger rising.

Bunz sat on Hideous' left leg while Butt-Butt sat on the right. His Cuban link brushed against Bunz's juicy titties, causing her to run her fingers across the iced-out letters.

"What do Hideous stand for?" she asked. "Yo name or sum?" She added.

"Yeah, lil' mama," he replied looking at Butt-Butt's huge ass grinding back and forth on top of him.

Shoota Face stepped up smelling heavily of weed with five bricks of ones in his hand. Bossman D Low's hit song *Shake Dat Ass* blared from the speakers. "To you thirsty, broke hoes!" He made it rain dead presidents all over her. Then to make it worse, he grabbed the Don Julio bottle and poured it all on Bunz.

She quickly jumped up in a rage. "What the fuck!" Bunz went straight up to him and got in his face. But Shoota Face was turnt up and he continued to throw money in the air.

"Meet me around back," Butt-Butt said, leaning back so he could hear her over the loud ass music pumping through the speakers.

"He don't like me, but his bitch love me!" Shoota Face was so lit he was rapping the lyrics with his eyes closed, throwing money into the air that he didn't see Hideous and Butt-Butt creep off together.

CHAPTER 13

Fireworks

Hideous pulled to the back of the club. As soon as he was about to roll up a blunt, the back exit door opened, and Butt-Butt walked out wearing a black bodysuit that looked like a scuba diving suit.

Butt-Butt got into the BMW whip all smiles and said, “I got a surprise for you.”

Before he could respond, the back door re-opened and out came Bunz wearing a skintight, strapless dress.

“Say, yo’ friend got me fucked up!” she spat, getting into the car. “Bitch ass nigga can’t get mad; he’s not my man.”

Before Hideous could even pull off, Butt-Butt’s hands were inside his jeans. She wrapped it around his rock-hard dick. And before he knew it, she had it in her mouth.

“Fuck that feels good!”

She couldn’t help but kiss all over it while she sucked it down her throat. She tried to put to shame every bitch who’d ever sucked his dick. She worked his dick and swallowed him whole.

“Damn, bitch, save me some,” Bunz said as she climbed to the front.

Inside Hideous’ BMW i8, the windows were steamy, and the show was on. Hideous had Butt-Butt on top, riding his dick in the backseat while Bunz recorded it in the front. She looked over her shoulder at the camera and began bouncing up and down on the dick faster, her ass jiggling a lot with each stroke. He squeezed an ass cheek in each hand and watched the dick slide in and out of her pussy. She had a dragon tattooed on her back.

He slapped her ass and screamed, "Fuck yeah."

They fucked like two wild dogs in heat. Bunz recorded the action while making her ass cheeks bounce in a rhythm, causing her dress to rise over her large ass completely. Hideous looked at Bunz's ass jump for a good minute before he lifted Butt-Butt off him.

"Bitch, just don't look. Come ride this dick," Hideous spat, swinging his dick back and forth in the air. He sat shirtless with sweat running down his body with his Cuban link danced like Mike Jack on his neck.

Bunz's pussy got wetter. She loved a man who took charge. Now Butt-Butt watched as her homegirl rode the dick like a cowgirl.

After a while, Bunz needed some air.

"This car is too small for all this ass," she moaned, biting on Hideous' right ear. She rode faster and reached down and tickled his balls while she rubbed her clit.

"So, what you saying, love?" Hideous asked. She showed him better than she could tell him.

With the butterfly door up and Versace Runners resting on the pavement, Hideous was leaning back on the side of his car, ramming in and out of Bunz from behind, right there outside on the side of the club.

"Dam, Bunz," said Butt-Butt, holding the phone sideways.

Bunz's ass was jigglin' with every stroke. Hideous' hands were held tight to her small waist, back and forth he rammed her. He was hitting her so hard that his nails dug deep into her flesh. He massaged her asshole with his thumb. She backed up right onto his thumb. And he fucked her hard until she couldn't take it no more.

"I can't take it! Damn! I can't take it." Bunz moaned trying to run free like a runaway slave.

"Damn! Bitch, let me show you how it's done." Butt-Butt grabbed Hideous' dick and filled her pussy with every inch.

WHAM! WHAM! WHAM!

She threw that ass back like a pro football quarterback. Hideous gripped her small waist; she had the biggest ass he'd ever seen, and he'd seen a lot of porn.

He had just taken the top two dreams off his "unfulfilled dreams" list in a single night.

He reached around and grabbed her tits, squeezing her nipples.

"Damn, I'm 'bout to nut all over yo' dickkk, fuccckkk!"

Hideous looked down and saw his dick covered in cum—his milky dick.

"Oh shit, oh shit." Hideous mumbled, feeling his own nut about to explode. He pulled out just in time and nutted on two gigantic assess that were twerking in front of him. His nut squirted out like a bottle of champagne.

"I'm gon' meet you back in the club, daddy. I know they probably looking all over for us." Butt-But said, picking up her bodysuit from the hood of the car.

"Damn, bitch, I'm surprise nobody walked out that hoe. I was scared as fuck. I thought they was going to see a real-life porno." Bunz chuckled, pulling her dress over her wide ass.

Hideous had to step back to admire Butt-Butt's round ass. He still couldn't believe he had fucked the two baddest bitches in the club.

Just before she pulled the suit over her ass, she brought her hands down to cuff her huge ass. She spread them apart and released her grip. It jiggled like a tennis ball. "Just a lil show to keep you thinking about me while you are laying up with yo' bitch tonight," she said, then stood on her tippy toes and made her ass move in circles like a washing machine, before pulling the bodysuit comfortably over her ass.

"Damn!" Hideous said, tilting his head to the side to get a better view.

CHAPTER 14

Club Shooting

Val sat at the barstool half naked with her ass hanging off the small circular stool. She knew she needed to get off her ass and find a trick to pay her bills. She scanned through the crowded club for a trick she could pop that ass for.

Val been stripping at DG's now for a couple of days. She was working the morning shift, but with a face and ass like hers, the manager immediately changed her to nights. This was her first Big Money Monday; Dallas vs. Houston Edition, and there was plenty of money in the building. But she hasn't made close to the money she needed for herself and son.

Val pushed her hair behind her ear and kept looking around the club.

"Bitch, you need to get up off that donkey ass of yours and chase that bread," Scream said walking up to the bar. "Give me two Lemon Drops, Butter," Scream said as she looked over at Val.

They had become friends after Crazy Red's funeral. At first Val thought she was one of Crazy Red's hoes, the way she was crying. Then she put two and two together, remembering Crazy Red mentioned Hideous having a twin sister. Scream was the one who convinced Val to strip.

At the word *money*, Val got really curious. "And what do you do?"

"Give me a call one day and find out," Scream said with a wink.

"I sat yo' drank right there." Scream pointed to the table where she had sat the drink next to Val's gold bra.

"I got to get back to this cash flow. You wanna sit there when all these tricks in this bitch, be my guess." Scream strolled off, wobbling her two yella ass cheeks to the Montana 700 pumping through the speakers.

Val stood and grabbed her bra. She snapped it back on and looked around the club for a potential victim, not knowing her night was about to go terribly wrong.

As soon as Hideous walked back into the packed club his eyes locked in on a fat, juicy ass that was all tatted up. He knew he had seen them tats before. Then it hit him.

Val was so focused on finding a trick that she didn't hear Hideous creep up behind her.

"Val, when you started stripping?" he asked, looking her up and down.

Val spun around and paused when she looked back and saw Hideous standing there. "Oh my God! I was just talking to yo—" She paused knowing Hideous didn't know his sister was a stripper. She played their conversation over and over in her head.

"A stripper! But why? Reuben and Chris out here having they way. You don't got to strip. I know yo' bro looking out."

"Bitch, I'm independent. I don't look for handouts. My brother does his thing and I do mines. But don't get a bitch wrong, he still spoiled my ass." She joked.

"So, how does he feel about you stripping? From what Chris used to tell me about Reuben, he can be overprotective over yo' ass. I can't believe he—"

Scream cut her off. "Bitch, I'm grown. I do what the fuck I want, and he don't need to know. You get what I'm saying? Keep your mouth shut." She warned.

"I mean, I was just thinking about you and Chris." She said, "Somebody got to pay the bills. It's been real hard since my Chris died, you know."

"I told you to call me if you ever needed something. I told ya' I got ya', and I mean that," he said, eyeballing every inch of her.

Val stood there topless in only a pair of heels and a gold thong bikini set. He had never pictured seeing her half naked like this. He stared at her camel toe.

Val felt uncomfortable by the way her deceased baby daddy's best friend was staring at a hole between her legs as if he had on some night vision goggles. She shifted her body to the side.

Hideous caught an eye full of her ass and mumbled "Damn, Val."

"What?" she asked, taken aback by Hideous' dick pressed up hard against his jeans, ready to bust out.

"You!" he said, stepping up into her space. He slid his hand inside her thong and rubbed her pussy.

She gripped his hand "What the fuck you doing, Reuben?"

"Bitch, don't you need this?" He pulled out a lot of money.

Seeing all the Ben Frank made her pussy jump.

Hideous slid a long finger all the way into her moist pussy. He began to fuck her pussy with his finger as he whispered all the things he wanted to do to her.

"Hold up. Chill. What about Chris?" she moaned above a whisper as his finger moved in and out of her super-soaked pussy.

"He's dead. He can't do shit about this." Feeling fucked up with his response she tried to remove his finger, but he pushed her hand away and continued to fuck her pussy. "Don't you need this money?" he asked again.

On the verge of busting her first nut since her BD's death, she tensed up. She couldn't lie; she needed the money. Just then she felt her orgasm take over her whole body. Her knees buckled and she almost fell, but Hideous caught her, feeling her up, touching every part of her body.

"What do you want from me?" she asked, feeling defeated by her greed for the money.

Hideous guided Val's small hand to his long dick. She had no choice but to submit. She wrapped her hands around it, and it felt like he had stolen one of the stripper poles and hid it down his pants. He guided her hand up and down on his inches.

"Hold up. Move close by the wall," he said as he led her to the darkest part in the club. He unzipped his pants and pulled out his dick. "What you gone do with all this?"

Val's eyes got bigger than a muthafucka. His dick was way bigger than Crazy Red's. "Oh my God," she whispered with her mouth in the shape of a letter "O".

"Give me what I want. And I'll give you what you want."

"But how?"

"Turn around and make it look like you twerking on that boy."

Val took a deep sigh and turned around with her back to him. She arched forward a little and pulled her thong to the side. He rubbed the end of his dick up and down her slit, wetting the head. Just when he was about to blow her back out, he snapped his head to see the fattest yella ass he done seen in the club all that night.

Then his look turned evil. He just spotted something in the club that fucked him up. His sister's pussy lips were hanging out the side of her G-string. "Man, move, bitch!" He pushed Val down on the floor and stormed off mad as fuck. On his way toward his twin, a tall, skinny nigga wearing skinny jeans bumped against him as he passed. "Damn, nigga watch where the fuck you going!" Hideous barked.

The tall, skinny dude turned and quickly got his mind right when he saw Hideous' hand patted his gun. "My fault, nigga." The tall, skinny dude put his hands up in the air.

"Pussy," Hideous mumbled through clenched teeth. He turned and kept moving through the crowd. "I know this stupid bitch not working up in this bitch."

Scream was so busy making her ass clap that she didn't see her brother until it was too late. She turned around at the last minute.

Hideous was so mad he yanked her by the arm. Scream knew her brother was throwed, but to embarrasse her like he did was inappropriate.

Icy Mike continued to hoot and holler with all his hood niggas. He thought maybe he was just a jealous boyfriend who came to rescue his hoe because he was damn sho trying to bag her. He continued to look in their direction. He was dragging her ass out by the arm. Yanking and pulling on her. Icy Mike's eyes widened, and his heart began to beat at a rapid pace when he saw Scream get slapped to the ground. He then realized that wasn't her boyfriend at all. He was her pimp, and he despised pimps. He watched his mama suffer at the hands of a pimp. Icy Mike already had it on his mind what he was going to do. He rushed toward the crowd trying to be Captain Save A Hoe. When he walked up, they were in a heated argument.

"Nigga, I know you didn't just put yo' muthafucking hands on me!" she yelled, pointing her finger all in her brother's face. If it was any other bitch, they would've been dead. Slumped over in a pool of blood.

"Say, my nigga, you didn't have to put yo' hands on her!" Icy Mike vented through clenched teeth.

"Gone on, lil' daddy, I got this," Scream said, trying to save his life.

"You sho, ma?"

"And if she wasn't?" Hideous barked, stepping up in Icy Mike's face. They were nose to nose.

"Say, you don't want these problems, my nigga!"

"Oh yeah." Hideous swung a haymaker that knocked Icy Mike back to one of the barstools.

The fight was now the main focus of the club. Strippers and hustlers looked on like it was the main event.

"Damnnn!" someone yelled from the crowd.

Hideous lunged and slammed Icy Mike's head down onto the bar counter. He then picked up a barstool and slammed it on his back.

"Say, that's Icy Mike fighting!" Corey C said as he ran to his hood nigga's aid with about seven more niggas behind him.

Corey C charged at Hideous, throwing hard punches that Hideous shoulder-rolled, and came back with a quick right to his chin, sending him crashing to the floor next to his broken rib partner.

"Hell naw! Ya'll not 'bout to jump my brother!" Scream yelled as she rushed over to help. She jumped on one of the niggas' backs, swinging wildly at his head.

Big BooBoo flipped her to the hard floor and started stomping her as if she was a nigga.

At that moment, four strippers jumped in the mix, including Val.

It was an all-out brawl. Stripper versus niggas.

Shoota Face had been looking at the fight from the side with everybody else. Scream locked eyes with him when she stood on wobbly legs.

WHAM!

A bitch out the crowd slept her from behind. Six big ass bouncers were trying to stop the big ass brawl, throwing hoes and niggas across the club. One of the massive bouncers tried to grab Hideous, which was a huge mistake. Hideous pulled out his Glock quick and smooth from his waistband.

"Oh shit!" the bouncer cried, jumping out of harm's way.

Hideous' eyes scanned the crowded club. The bouncers had cleared most of the damage, and his sister was back on her feet, but he didn't care about none of that. He wanted the bitch ass nigga that started all this shit. Not finding his intended target, he locked eyes with the clown ass nigga who bumped into him just a few minutes ago.

Hideous crept up on him with his gun close to his side. The crowd was too busy watching the bouncers throw whoever was involved in the riot out.

The tall skinny nigga followed his cousin's gaze, turning to face Hideous. "What the fuck?" he said, almost muttering the words under his breath.

Hideous didn't give him a chance to say anything else. He raised the gun, aimed toward his face and fired.

The shot tore through his face, practically tearing it off. Blood splattered as the side of his head exploded, the flesh shredded like raw cabbage. He stumbled sideways then hit the ground.

Hideous turned the gun onto the cousin and fired in his face too— his skull exploded in a mess of blood and brains and fragments of bones.

The homeboy they were with turned and ran like everybody else did once the shots got to firing. Hideous took aim. He lined up his shot with the pussy and pulled the trigger. The bullet slammed into the nigga's back, splattering his blood and causing him to drop.

The screams echoed off the club's walls as everybody ran and ducked for cover. People were stampeding toward the exit, fighting and fuckin' each other up as they shoved their way out the exits. Scream ran like the rest of them while her brother shot the bitch up. The tall, skinny nigga's homebody still couldn't believe he'd been shot. He was gasping for air as he looked up at the cold eyes of a killer. Hideous stood over him and placed the gun under his chin. He pulled the trigger before he could plea for mercy. The blast ripped through the top of his skull, blowing the top of his skull open. Some of his teeth had broken free of the gum and were floating in the pool of blood that had filled his mouth. It was quite a horrific sight.

***

When Hideous walked through the door, Caprice ran up to him and wrapped her arms around him. "What happened at the club? I'm so glad you are okay. I got a call from my homegirl saying a crazy muthafucka shot the whole place up."

"Why you didn't tell me my sister danced with you at DG's?"

Caprice stepped back and looked into his eyes. Right then she knew he was the one responsible for the murders. After the mayhem was over, three men were left for dead. "Come follow me, baby, let me explain," she begged grabbing his hand. She led him to the sofa. "Sit and relax, baby."

Caprice was wearing Hideous' favorite 2828 graphic shirt. She pulled the shirt over her head, dropping it to the floor, kicking it to the side. Butt ass naked she walked up to him and dropped to her knees. She unzipped his jeans.

Hideous threw his head back while Caprice ate him whole, but his mind was on finishing what he had started with Val. But first he had to call his business partner. It was time for him to open club Tip'z.

***

Shoota Face sat on the bed with no shirt, no boxers, just jewelry on. His phone lit up on the dresser. He reached for it and pressed the talk button. "Wassup, baby boy?"

"We need to link up tomorrow. A bunch shit went down tonight. I can't speak on phone about."

"I heard, broddy. I thought you left so I dipped out with shorty."

Shoota Face had crept out the club just before the shooting, right after Scream had gotten slept. He was dying laughing.

"Hell yeah, I knocked that hoe out. I never did like that Renni Rucci wannabe bitch," Big Booty Susie, spat walking out the restroom butt ass naked. She climbed on top Shoota Face and was about to give him the ride of his life.

CHAPTER 15

Silent Money

As soon as Uzi Mi's head lieutenant sat in front of the glass window that separated the two ruthless men, Uzi Mi got straight to the point. "Where is the money?"

"I'm on it. I've asked everybody in that damn neighborhood about anything unusual they seen that day. Nobody talking." Black Rhino said.

"I bet if we start murkin' shit over there they'll get their muthafuckin' minds right," Uzi Mi barked.

Black Rhino chuckled. It's been three months, and Uzi Mi still had that killer mentality. "But on some real shit, you sho you didn't see shit at all that day?" Black Rhino asked.

"Man, I told you a hundred times the only thing I seen that morning was a YN. He must have seen me when I hide them hoes."

"Just give me more time, I gotcha," Black Rhino promised.

"Muthafucka, you had three months! Don't worry though, in three weeks I'm out this hoe and I'm gone murk me some muthafuckas." With that, Uzi Mi stood and disappeared down the hall.

Black Rhino just shook his head, knowing the worst was about to come.

***

Two weeks after the club shooting Hideous opened up a strip club in a three-bedroom house. He named it Tip'z. It was in the basement of the house. It had one L-shaped stages and two poles. It was used for an afterhours spot where hoes could make extra money shaking. He also had a small bar and a DJ booth that sat on the side of the basement. Club Tip'z was literally the place to be. It had a bunch of bad bitches who Caprice had recruited, and a lot more who was literally begging Hideous to chew his dick off for them to work there.

Club Tip'z didn't have any rules. The strippers could fuck, suck, and smoke all the drugs they wanted as long as they paid their percentage at the end of the night. Hideous also always kept that White Girl on him.

Tonight, it was no different. Cars were lined up and down the block. Even unwanted guests were out looking to come up off the name Hideous.

"Yeah, that's him. That's the nigga that killed all our homies. Now he getting paid off our dead homies," Lil Mike Mike said, pointing at Hideous.

"You sho that's the muthafucka that killed Yella Kid?"

"Yeah, I'm positive."

Fat Al slanted his eyes at the man who killed his lil cousin. "Yeah, we gon' spin on that nigga tonight," he spat as he started up the stolen white Cown Vic. He slowly passed Hideous with murderous intentions.

"Damn, baby, who is that?" Caprice asked, straining her eyes but could not see inside the car because of the tint, but the driver's actions spoke louder than words.

Hideous threw up the middle finger at the passing whip while patting his gun that rested under his red 2828 shirt. "Fuck whoever it is. He just mad because his bitch inside my shit, making my pockets fat."

"Boy, shut up." Caprice walked up on him and pressed her mouth to his, just when he was blowing out the weed he consumed in his body. It went into her lungs and made her whole entire body numb. "I'm 'bout to go back in and make some of this money. You need to call yo' sista to see wassup with yo' money— why you keep coming up short every time."

"Yeah, you right."

"Get on that, bae, for real." Caprice walked off.

Hideous pulled hard on the weed before pulling out his iPhone 17 Pro Max. He had two missed calls and a text message from Val. Hideous scrolled with his index finger to the message icon and read the message.

BigbootyVal: You need to call me back. I know you see I been calling since yo' ass shot up the club. I want my money for the sneaky shit you pulled. You either call back, or you know what comes next!

Reply: Bitch, is you threatening me?

BigbootyVal: Call it what you want. I want my money.

Reply: Bitch, where you at? I'll bring it to you right now. Are you at home?

BigbootyVal: Nope. I'm at Chris' mama's house.

Reply: How long you gon' be over there?

BigbootyVal: Until she gets back from outta town. She took my baby to a family reunion. I'm watching her house for her.

Reply: So, you are all alone. Pinpoint me the addy. We got unfinished business, and you not getting shit until I bust this nut across yo' face, bitch!

Once Hideous got the addy, he called his sister.

She answered on the third ring. "Wassup, baby brother?"

"You tell me. Did you count that again?"

"Yeah, it added back with the same amount as before."

"What the fuck you mean, Rachel?"

"Like the fuck I said, Reuben. I done counted it twice, me and Jelly, but it keeps coming up short."

Scream was quickly cut off by her brother's rough but deep voice. "Why you got that bitch counting my money? She probably be the reason my shit coming up missing."

"Boy, shut the fuck up. Ever since you put yo' hands on me you been feeling yourself. You got me fucked up. You need to be asking yo' scary ass business partner what his count is."

"You know what? I'm on my way over there." CLICK!

"Hello? Reuben?" All Scream saw flash on her screen was *ENDED CALL*. "Say, bitch, my twin brother is on his way, and he's pissed the fuck off that we keep coming up a couple racks short."

"Damn!" Jelly said as she sucked on the end of the exotic blunt with pleasure. Pulling hard she added, "Do you and yo' twin look alike? Are y'all identical? I hope he likes me. How I look, bitch?" She stood, cuffin' her two juicy ass cheeks. "Damn, do you think my ass too big? Do he like a big ass, Ra—"

"Bitch, shut the fuck up, damn. And no, we look nothing alike. I told you before me and my twin was in a bad ass fire when we were younger and half his face is gone."

"Awww, what happened?"

Scream told her roommate everything. How Reuben could've saved himself, but instead he saved her. "He will forever be my hero," Scream said, blinking away the tears that threatened to fall down her face.

Jelly's mouth was dropped. She had never heard a deeper story.

"Bitch, pick ya lip up off yo' titty. My brother good. He ain't ugly or nun. He just got scars."

"Naw, bitch, that story was deep. I admire him."

"Bitch, shut the fuck up and get yo' lil boyfriend up outta here. If my brother sees him, it's gon' be some mo' shit."

As soon as Hideous walked back into the crowded house, he walked down the steps that led him into Club Tip'z. He looked around the small basement. On the right side of the L-shaped stage was pussy in full view. A slim stripper with enough ass for days was sliding down the pole, legs wide open in a full split. On the right side, a red bone horse-built stripper was standing on her head, leaning against the pole, making that ass wiggle and pussy pop.

He continued to search for Caprice's ass until his eyes finally rested on her. She was on the main stage that sat in the center. "That's why I didn't see the bitch; everybody surrounding her," Hideous said out loud as he watched her put on for the club.

She grabbed both of her titties and squeezed them juicy muthafuckas together while she squatted that 45-inch ass over a Ciroc bottle. With piles of money at her feet she spread her pussy lips slowly apart and slowly slid down the bottle until the top half disappeared. With the bottle deep inside her, she stood and bounced that ass like she had something to prove. She then sat on a metal folded chair behind her. She inserted the bottle back into her wetness and slowly moved it in and out of her opening without using her hands. The hustlers, drug dealers, rappers, and bad bitches all threw more money on Caprice. Once she blew everybody's mind, including Hideous', she gave a big push.

THUNK! She let the bottle drop to the floor. More money was poured, and more phones were out recording all the fun at club Tip'z.

Caprice gathered all her things and cleaned up all the dead presidents that were scattered all over the stage with her pink G-string laying on top. She had to admit she made more money at Club Tip'z than anywhere else in the city. Once she was done, she wrapped a towel around her nakedness and withdrew to the back of the club.

Hideous looked at his phone to check the time—something he didn't have. "Butter, do me a favor," he said to a waitress that was built like one of the strippers down in the basement.

She had ass and big o' titties. She stood there naked as the day she was born and danced under the dim light. She moved her wide hips in a slow, circular motion. "Yeah, wassup, baby?" she said, holding a tray full of two-dollar shots.

"Tell Caprice I had to go check in with my sister about that issue."

"Oh, tell her I said I miss making her favorite drinks back at the old club." Butter licked her tongue over her sexy lips, causing her tongue ring to rub against them sexy muthafuckas.

"I will. Just hold my spot down. Make sho nobody kill nobody." Hideous joked staring at her hourglass figure. "When you gone stop serving dranks and start making some real money in this bitch?"

"Hold up, you bet to believe…*ouch*! Hold this for me." She handed him the tray. "Fuck! these hoe ass nipple rings be aggravating a bitch," she spat, pulling on her nipple to re-adjust the rings that were pierced between her flesh. "Okay, much better, but like I said a bitch be making her munyun serving drinks. Hell, I might be making more than these stanky ass bitches off in here!" she hissed, taking the tray from Hideous.

"I'm just saying, all this ass…" He smacked her ass, causing a tidal wave somewhere. "…Can get a shit load of cash. I'm just saying, but I got to go. Tell Caprice that for me."

"Bet," she said as Hideous watched her disappear in the crowd.

3:00 a.m.

As soon as Hideous walked out of the house, his phone began to vibrate. It was a message from Val. He clicked on it.

BigbootyVal: You need to bring yo' ass like right now with my money. You know what? Let me make a phone call to 9-11.

Reply: Bitch you wanna play? I'm on my way, hoe!"

BigbootyVal: If you're not here in the next twenty minutes, the police will be knocking Club Tip'z door down tonight. Yeah, bitch. I also know all about it. Club Tip'z located in one of yo' spots in the Cliff. Play with me if you want.

Hideous took a deep breath and let out a long ass sigh. He texted his sister, telling her he'll be there a lil later. He got in his BMW i8 that was parked in front and drove off, heading toward Cedar Hill.

CHAPTER 16

Never Be The Same

Hideous pulled up in front of Crazy Red's mama's four-bedroom house in Cedar Hill, parking backwards in the empty driveway. He grabbed his Uzi machine. He adjusted the Cuban link chain that hung from his neck like a chandelier and stepped out into the night's cool breeze. A second later, he rang the doorbell.

The door was snatched open. "Where the fuck is my money!" Val said as she answered the door wearing a wine-colored silk kimono open enough in the front to show him plenty of her beautiful, round tits. From the appealing way those bitches bounced as she walked, he knew she wasn't wearing a bra. A matching cloth belt secured the kimono around her slender waist.

SMACK!

Val lost her balance and fell hard to the floor.

"*Bitch*! Don't never threaten me." Hideous yelled as he reached down and grabbed her by the hair, yanking and smacking her again.

"What the fuck!" she yelled. He started to choke her for her disrespect like she owed him money.

When he released his Kungfu grip from around her neck, he slapped her again across the face, sending her crashing back to the floor.

"Okay! Okay! I'm sorry," she said, making it to her hands and knees.

Hideous turned and was about to leave when Val stopped him.

"Reuben." She stood, making it to her feet.

"Wassup?" he said through clenched teeth. As usual, he couldn't keep his eyes off of her bountiful tits.

"I need that money!" she pleaded.

"Once I nut in yo' face you can get it. Until then, don't call me for shit. And if I feel like you even pass the police station, I'll kill you," he promised.

"Hold up, come here."

Hideous stepped into the neatly furnished house and set his gun by the door.

She led him to the kitchen and handed him a glass of red wine. "I need that money."

"Well, you know what you got to do to get it."

Val let the robe drop to the floor. She was standing in front of him wearing nothing but a gold necklace her baby daddy got her just before he was killed. She paraded in front of him, swaying her hips. She walked him to the living room where she sat on the couch. She leaned back on the sofa and grabbed her legs behind her knees and jerked them up to her tits, shamelessly exposing herself.

Soon the house was echoing with lustful groans and moans. He fucked her quite a while right there on the sofa. He pounded her for a good fifteen minutes, grunting with each fierce stroke. She bucked her hips up and down and thrashed her head from side to side, and her big tits rolled back and forth on her chest.

"I'm cumming!" she cried.

That turnt Hideous up. He began fucking her with long, slow strokes. He leaned forward and put her legs on his shoulders so he could plunge in even deeper. He hammered her hard. He pulled out, and then slammed it back in.

"Your dick is too big. What was I thinking? Please tell me you're close to cumming!"

"A few more minutes!"

"Ahheeuuu!" she screamed. "Pull out… It's too much!"

After a while, she told him to let her catch her breath. She stood to her feet with her pussy hurting.

Hideous' dick was about to explode at the sight in front of him. Val was booty ball naked, pussy dripping wet with her cum.

"Follow me," she said, ass jiggling with her every step like she was twerking that fat muthafucka.

As he followed her to the master bedroom, he stared at Val's ass and shook his head. She had more ass fat on her ass than anywhere else on her body. After having Lil' Chris, Val's ass and thighs expanded. Everybody thought she had ass shots like every other bitch with a fat ass, but not Val. It was all her.

When they entered the large master bedroom, they got straight to it. Hideous' jeans were already hanging off his butt, showing off his Gucci boxers, dick sticking straight up out the designer brand.

"Get down and eat this dick."

Val looked down hungrily at all the cash in Hideous' hand. She sucked her teeth, not wanting to suck her baby daddy's best friend's dick, but she was weak for a dead president. She wrapped her soft hands around his long dick and began to stroke it. She managed to get him all the way down her throat.

Grabbing her head from the back, he pumped into her mouth, beating her face in. Hideous watched as his dick disappeared down her throat. He started pumping into her mouth like a jack rabbit. Her hazel eyes were staring up at him with tears threatening to fall. She was trying her hardest not to gag. Hideous pulled his dick from her mouth for a second and grabbed her juicy titties. He watched as his dick got swallowed up by them two juicy muthafuckas. He held her titties in his hands while his dick slid up and down her chest. He pinched and pulled at her nipples, then shoved his dick back into her wet mouth.

She sucked vigorously, head moving back and forth. She wanted to bite his dick off, but she thought about her baby and kept on sucking. It felt like an hour when he finally told her to stop.

She cut her eyes at him in disgust and rolled them.

"Do yo' duty and ride that dick. Don't stop until you bust or I bust." He demanded.

She placed her hands on her thick thigh and rode him like an award-winning jockey. Up and down, she bounced, ass smacking off Hideous' thighs.

SMACK! SMACK! SMACK!

After twenty minutes of riding non-stop, she slowly spun around with his dick still inside of her. With her back toward him she started again, ass jiggling with every bounce. He stared at her ass, then got stuck on her tatted up back. He read *R.I.P. Chris*, big with the date he was born, sunrise: 10-25-94, and the date he died, sunset: 7-27-25.

Hideous shook his head. It ain't even been a whole month yet. He continued to scan her. Tattoos covered her whole entire back. He saw a portrait of Crazy Red holding his son on the far-left side of her lower back. Hideous had to shut his eyes, not wanting to see his best friend smiling up at him, or the fact that his BM's ass was slapping against his balls every time she landed. At that moment he realized hoes weren't shit. All for the paper she had sold her soul to the devil.

SMACK! SMACK! SMACK! SMACK!

Hideous opened his eyes and stared at nothing but ass and tattoos. He reached out to spread one of her chunky cheeks and stuck a finger into her ass. She gasped and squeezed her titties together with both hands while biting down on her bottom lip.

She stopped bouncing and was now grinding all the way down, back and forth on his monster. She felt it all in her stomach. She closed her eyes and threw her head back and moaned.

4:45a.m.

"Just leave my money on the bed and please leave. I gave you my body," she hissed as she climbed out the bed with the sheet pulled in front of her exposed titties and bald pussy, leaving the back exposed for the world to see.

Hideous laid there with his dick in the air. "Damn, bitch, you gone take the sheet with ya?" he spat, looking at Val's ass jiggle all the way out the room.

"For real, you need to be gone by the time I get back," Val hurled over her shoulder.

Back at Club Tip'z

5:00a.m.

"Listen, we're 'bout to leave out this bitch. Are you coming with me or not?" Moneybag TT asked as he popped another bottle of champagne and headed over where his two niggas were standing.

"Yeah, hold up, though. Let me call my homegirl so she can come, too."

"Well, hurry up," he said, an uninterested tone in his voice. He turned toward the crowd and made it rain more hundred-dollar bills.

Caprice called Scream while looking at Moneybag TT throw money like it grew off trees. Scream didn't pick up so Caprice called again.

She answered on the fourth ring. "Damn, bitch, it's five in the fuckin' morning. What?"

"Say, I need you. I got us one up in here throwing money like he owns a bank or somethin'." Caprice said.

"Bitch, do you see what time it is? And, plus, Reuben is on his way over here."

"Damn. He still ain't made it over there yet?"

"Naw, he texted me earlier saying he'll be over later on."

"He might be laid up with a bitch. I swear niggas ain't shit, but let's get this money. I'm leaving with this nigga in a minute. He's waiting for me. I promise this will be the last lick for the Wolfpack."

"Ugh, okay, send me the addy."

"See, bitch, that's why I love you. Let's get this munyun and bring yo' roommate, for real."

"Hold up, why?"

"Because it's three of them, but I got it under control. Shit ain't going to go bad like it did for you and Molly. I'm bringing Butter just in case."

"The waitress from DG's?"

"Yeah, bitch, Butter look good. She got a body and a ass big as hell. She is about as bad as you. I know it's gon' be a piece of cake. Watch. But I got to go. Here come ol' dude." She hung up.

Moneybag TT came up from behind Caprice and wrapped his arm around her body. "You ready to go?" he whispered as he palmed her whole pussy.

"Oooh, shit, that feels good!" Caprice moaned.

"Say, BB 1000, let's bounce, dawg."

BB 1000 grabbed Butter's hand and pulled her toward the exit with Moneybag TT and the rest of the crew right behind them.

5:25a.m.

Later, after Val took a quick shower, she came back into the master bedroom to find Hideous sitting on the edge of the bed. "Damn, you still here? You need to go, for real," Val spat with venom in her tone. She looked him up and down while she snapped back on her bra.

He pulled his designer hoodie over his head, grabbed his bussdown and baby Uzi from the dresser. He was about to leave when Val stopped him.

"Hold up, where's my money?"

Hideous pulled out a big wad of cash from his front hoodie pocket. He threw it up like he was a pitcher in the major leagues. Money flew everywhere.

"Really? That shit was so childish."

"Who the fuck you got in my house, girl?" Lady Love was saying but was caught by surprise when she seen Hideous getting dressed.

They both jumped in surprise.

"So, this is how y'all pay my son's memory back?"

"Look, I can explain," Val said as tears fell down her face, but she would never get the chance to finish.

She watched as Lady Love's head exploded as the bullets from the Uzi rained into her face. Val screamed and covered her mouth. Half her head was shredded, reduced to nothing more than a crimson smudge on the wall.

He raised the Uzi and pointed it at her face and spat, "I killed Chris because I caught him fuckin' my sister!"

BUDDABUDAA! BUDDABUDDA!

Val's eyes got big and not from the bullets that filled her up with holes all in the face and upper body.

Hideous wiped down the place real good then went through Lady Love's Prada bag. He took her money and left out the front door, leaving Lil' Chris crying his eyes out.

5:45 a.m.

At The Omni Hotel

As soon as they entered the presidential suite, Butter pushed the straps off her designer dress, allowing the flimsy dress to drop to the floor. She thrusted her melons out proudly and paraded in front of them, swaying her hips seductively.

"Rachel, I don't have to take off my clothes, right?" Jelly asked innocently, looking at Butter throw her ass every time she took a step.

"Damn, that bitch ass fat than a bitch," one of Moneybag TT's niggas boasted.

"I know. Right, Killa K? And this all me right here," BB 1000 said cupping both of Butter's ass cheeks so everyone could see she was all his.

But she walked up and stopped in front of Killa K, ran a finger along her slit, and put it in his mouth. “I can be with whoever. Let’s get this shit started.” She scrambled to her knees in the center of the room, had all three men stand in a circle and sighed. “Ummm, I want to suck some dick.”

“What? I thought we were coming here to chill.” Jelly watched as Butter serviced all three men.

Moneybag TT and Killa K were both on the big side, and she had a bit of trouble swallowing them. She managed to get Killa K all the way down her throat.

“Bitch we gon’ do what we do, and we gone make this munyun, you hear me?”

“Yeah, I hear you, but I have never done this type of shit before,” Jelly said in a lighter whisper.

“Is everything alright? I’m ‘bout to go join Butter. She over there sucking dick by herself. What y’all gon’ do?”

“This bitch acting all scared.” Scream spat with a sour look on her face.

“Bitch, you better make some money; all that ass you got. Better quit playing. Scream, I’m about to go fuck and suck these niggas. What you gon’ do?”

“Hold up, I’m ‘bout to be over there. Let me get her straight first.”

“Okay,” Caprice said as she aggressively threw her ass as she went over where Butter was sucking all three dicks. She had jaws of steel. Each nigga had his head thrown back.

“You ready, bitch?” Scream asked, wiggling out of her tight ass leggings, letting her meaty ass jiggle out of the thin fabric.

“Yeah, let’s go,” Killa K mumbled under his breath. He took a seat on the all-white sofa and pulled his designer pants completely off. He was the first to cum in Butter’s mouth, now he wanted Scream.

Jelly looked at Scream taking off her blouse, so she followed suit. She squeezed her big, chocolate ass out of her jeans. She wore nothing but a lime green thong. Her meaty ass caused Killa K's eyes to expand. He had to be dreaming. Both bitches were out of this world bad, and he had them all to himself

"Play some music," Scream said.

Killa K grabbed his iPhone 17 and browsed through his playlist and put on his favorite song by Bossman DLow. *Shake Dat Ass* filled the room.

Without hesitation Scream started shaking her ass. Scream's ass was so big that each time it made contact it would bounce from one cheek to the other. "You like that, baby?" she whispered seductively.

"Hell yeah!"

Jelly sat next to Killa K as he was sipping on his cup of Muddy Sprite.

Later...

Moneybag TT was laid out on the king size bed at one of the best five-star hotels in Dallas with one of the baddest bitches at Club Tip'z. She was sucking his dick like she had a V8 motor attached to the side of her mouth. On the side of him was his cousin BB 1000. He was receiving the ride of his life by a slippery wet pussy. Butter bounced that ass on him reverse cowgirl. She was literally giving both men a lot to see as her fat, bubble booty bounced and bounced.

"Daddy, we can leave them here while me and you go have some fun with the other two big booty hoes. What you say about that?" Caprice whispered with cum dripping down her chin.

"I say let's do it, but what about my other nigga?"

"You don't see all this ass? She can handle two dicks. One in her pussy the other one in her mouth or her ass. Ain't that's right, bitch?" Caprice slapped Butter's ass, leaving it red and stinging.

"Yessss! Shit, yes!" Butter cried into the pillow.

CHAPTER 17

Sex, Sweat, & Tears

When Caprice and Moneybag TT walked back into the living room, Caprice was shocked to see Jelly's face buried in Killa K's lap. Her head doing a repeat; up, down, up and down. She deep throated his dick long and wet while his index finger dug deep into her tight ass.

Scream sat and watched as her roommate ate the dick like it was her last meal.

"Damn, bitch, I thought she was shy. I guess not." Caprice chuckled.

Jelly stuck her middle finger up while she continued to suck dick like she had something to prove. A minute later, she swallowed every drop of Killa K's seed with ease.

After watching his young soldier bust a nut in the chocolate bitch's mouth his dick was so hard, he quickly kicked off his Jay's and took off all his clothes so fast that it would've set a new world record.

He stared at Caprice who was laying spread eagle in the middle of the king-sized bed, squeezing her titties and rubbing her fat clit.

"You got to fuck her first, and make it hard…" Caprice said as she closed her legs shut. "…*if* you want some of this good pussy." She re-opened her legs and stuck a finger in her sloppy wet pussy.

Moneybag TT couldn't take his eyes off her fat pussy. She closed her legs, and he zeroed in on Jelly. She raised her hips and let him remove her lime green thong. While he tore open the gold wrapped condom, he watched Scream intensely stick one finger after another in Caprice's pussy until three of her fingers were going in and out all at the same time.

Once the condom was rolled on, he positioned himself between Jelly's thick, chocolate legs. "Damn, y'all turning me on," Moneybag TT said. She was now bent over headfirst smacking on Caprice's pussy.

He flipped Jelly on her stomach while staring at Scream's colorful ass and her fat pussy.

Jelly closed her eyes as Moneybag TT grabbed her slim waist and stroked deep inside her. He thrusted long and hard, forcing Jelly to make all type of sex faces. He pounded in her while staring hard at Scream shake her enormous ass cheeks together that made a loud clapping sound.

Jelly tried to run from that dick. "Fuckkk! Fuccck!" she cried as she shut her eyes tight.

Once Scream was done tongue-kissing Caprice's pussy, both women crawled seductively over to watch the action that was going on before them.

SQUEAK! SQUEAK! SQUEAK!

Sweat and tears ran down Jelly's face. He long-dicked her body way from Loop 12 causing her body to shake and tremble at the same damn time.

"Ahhhhh fuck!" Once her orgasm passed through her body, she opened her eyes to find Caprice in front of her with her legs wide open, pussy smiling back at her.

"Yeah, take that dick!" Scream said, grabbing Jelly by the hips, forcing her to throw it back harder on Moneybag TT's dick.

"You like that, bitch," Moneybag TT roared, slapping the shit outta Scream's bare ass, leaving it red.

Caprice buried Jelly's face in her pussy, and moved her hips in a circular motion while Scream's hands were still pushing her hips up against the dick.

"Fuuuuuuucccccckkkk!" Jelly screamed, face moist with Caprice's juices all over her mouth and chin.

Scream removed her hands from Jelly's tiny waist, causing her to collapse between Caprice's legs.

Moneybag TT got in the push up position and pounded as hard as he could into Jelly's tight pussy. Once he was tired of Jelly, he positioned himself behind Scream. She knew what it was. She lay faced down, ass up, arching her back just right for him.

"Make that bitch big booty clap." Caprice moaned.

Moneybag TT fucked Scream's ass until she couldn't take it anymore. "Hold up, I'm 'bout to bust. Fuccckkk!" Moneybag TT roared.

"Let us clean up. We gon' be out to clean you up in a minute."

"Bitch, you got me fucked up!" Scream stared at Caprice who had a smirk on her face. "You draw down. This yo' lick." They were arguing on who was gon' draw down.

A second later, Caprice came back holding a chrome .25 with a pink pearl handle.

"Hold up bitch, what you doing," Jelly snapped, moving out the way.

"Whoa! Hold up, what you got going?" Moneybag TT spat, raising his voice. He attacked her, grabbing her by the throat and slamming her into the bathroom, smashing her head over on the mirror. He grabbed a shard of broken glass and slashed her throat. It happened so fast Scream didn't know what to do.

Jelly screamed and screamed, not believing what she was seeing.

Scream, on the other hand, rushed and snatched up the chrome .25 and aimed it at Moneybag TT. She pulled the trigger twice, hitting him in the chest. Blood-spattered all over Jelly. She screamed some more.

Without thinking twice, Scream grabbed a badly shaken up Jelly and quickly took off running out the room with her gun aimed and ready. BB 1000 and Killa K had thrown their hands in the air. Butter grabbed her things and all three women ran out the house.

"Bitch, what are we going to do? I can't go to jail!" Jelly cried. They sat inside of Caprice's 2025 Kia 5.

"Bitch, pull it together. Everything happened so fast. It didn't supposed to go like that." She couldn't believe her best friend was dead.

CHAPTER 18

Welcome Home

One week later

Black Rhino still hadn't run into the YN Uzi Mi claimed he almost ran over the day of the bank robbery. But he did get a helpful tip. He found out the mystery boy came up on a bunch of money.

"Yeah, Reuben is his name," Ms. Parker informed, smoking a Newport short.

"So, you seen him that morning running from the scene?"

"Yeah, I don't got to lie about that shit. He is always in some shit. He done bought him a Cybertruck and some mo shit. I know it was something," she replied, flicking the cigarette butt to the ground.

"Where can I find him?"

"Damn, you the police or sum? You pulled up at my front porch in a 20," she pondered looking at the SUV in awe.

"2025."

"Damn! 2025 for real, well, a 2025 Escalade. What's in it for me, a reward or some?" She said, placing her hand on her wide hips.

Black Rhino laughed out loud. "Hell naw. I'm not no muthafuckin' popo. I'm just looking for the lil nigga."

"And what's yo' reason?" She shifted her wide hips to the opposite side.

"Look, here." Black Rhino peeled off five Ben Franks and handed it to her. She quickly snatched the money and stuffed it down her bra.

"Now, we're talking. His lil ugly ass use to stay over there with his mama and twin sister, but what I hear, he done moved them out to the suburbs and shit," she said pointing at a boarded-up house next to hers.

"Anything else you can tell me?"

"I know one thing he got that munyun now."

"Thank you for ya help, ma'am," Black Rhino peeled off five mo Ben Franks before getting back in the Escalade.

Dallas County Jail Monday
7:02 a.m.

"Say, I got some good news for you. The nigga we're looking for name is Reuben. His sister is a famous stripper in the city named Scream. I talked to somebody that know them, know them."

Uzi Mi cut him off. "Look his sister up on the Gram. I know the bitch got a picture of her brother on her page."

"Hold up, I see a picture of a dark-skinned nigga with the caption reads: My other half. My brother. There go his page: @Hideous!_makeitrainCash."

Black Rhino went to Hideous' page and seen only one picture. The same one that was on his sister's page. "I see the same picture of him. You can't really see the nigga's face. He's sitting in a chair with two bad bitches sitting in his lap. He got his face buried in one of the bad bitches' chest."

"Screenshot the picture and save in yo' phone. Do you know what today is?"

"Your bond hearing."

"Exactly, I been in this bitch for ninety days with a million-dollar bond. They got to lower it today."

9:00 a.m.
a few hours later

Uzi Mi waited in the courtroom hold over for his bond hearing. He had no worries. He been sitting with a high ass bond set at a million. His lawyer promised him they could get it lowered in ninety days. His wait was over.

"Uzziel Michaels, let's go!" A broad-shouldered deputy ordered, handcuffing his hands in front of him.

The deputy led Uzi Mi through an adjacent door where the courtroom was located. "I hope they bury yo' funky ass, nigger!" The redneck barked.

"If they don't just know while you're here working hard, I'll be working extra harder fuckin' ya wife in her pink tight ass!" Uzi Mi chuckled before he got shoved into the courtroom.

The courtroom was packed on both sides. On one side the victim's family sat; on the other side, his T. Jones and granny sat in front with their Black Lives Matter T-shirts on with a picture of his older brother on the front.

Uzi Mi smiled in their direction as the bailiff escorted him to his seat.

"All rise for the Honorable Judge Johnson," the older black bailiff announced.

Uzi Mi stood alongside his lawyer with a big smile written across his face. An older black man with gray hair walked in glaring at the young man before him.

The Judge shuffled through the papers before saying, "Everybody can be seated." He looked over the papers on last time and said, "I see Mr. Michael's you been incarcerated for over ninety days now and the state of Texas has granted your bond reduction to be set from one million dollars to two hundred and fifty thousand dollars.

"What the fuck!" One of the victim's family members screamed.

"Order in my courtroom!" the Judge roared.

The Judge announced in a firm voice, glaring at Uzi Mi. "The court had adjourned. You all can be dismissed!" He then banged the gavel letting a ruthless killer back on the streets. It was an uproar inside the courtroom. The victim's family grieved while his family hugged.

Uzi Mi sat there with a big smile plastered across his face. He looked over at his mama and read her lips, "Welcome home."

CHAPTER 19

Trust No One

Uzi Mi lived in a beautiful all white mansion on the outskirts of Dallas in Frisco. The mansion was called the White House because it is identical to the in Washington D.C, but without all the extra guards and other bullshit inside.

Inside Uzi Mi's was six bedrooms, nine bathrooms, an indoor basketball court and a big ass living room with a huge gold chandelier that hung just above the wide dining room table.

Uzi Mi was only twenty-six living next door to doctors and lawyers. His neighbors thought he was a rapper or some shit, but he made his money off the streets. He made his first $200 thousand dollars robbing an armor truck at the age of seventeen. After that, he never looked back. He went from robbing armored trucks to robbing banks and as you can see, life was going well for him. Until he brought his older brother Red Ronnie to a bank job he regrets doing.

Red Ronnie was a hot head, always ready to bust them thangz. He was recently released from the Feds for a jewelry heist that went terribly wrong. Two men were killed and unfortunately for him, he was shipped to serve a 15-year sentence.

Flip, Monster B, and three lil bad bitches were baggin' up some pills. As they were bagging up, Uzi Mi appeared in the room with no shirt on. He was heavily tatted, smoking on some Za. He looked at the three half naked hoes, not because they were all bad bitch material, but to make sho none of them tried to steal from him. He stood on business.

"What you got in yo' mouth, bitch?"

"Nothing! I swear!" She said quickly.

"Open yo' mouth, bitch!" She did as she was told. He examined her mouth from top to bottom then shoved one of the nines in her mouth so hard that it chipped her front tooth. "Bitch, did you swallow it! Did you swallow my pill?"

"No, I promise!" She gagged.

"Boss, chill you gone scare the bitches off," Flip joked.

BOOM!

Uzi Mi shot Flip in the kneecap. Flip grabbed his knee and rock back and forth like a bitch going in labor on the floor.

"Ahhhhhhhhhh!" He screamed in severe pain.

"Get back to work. It ain't no time for a fuckin' break." He snapped.

Black Rhino entered the house with five YNs close behind him. Black Rhino stepped over the man as if he wasn't even there.

"I found the bitch. I know where Reuben's sister at. She is attending TWU out there in Denton," Black Rhino confirmed.

"Well, let's make a surprise visit, Monster B, go get them choppers. We 'bout to rain bullets in Denton, Texas."

***

Hideous pulled up in front of Shoota Face mama's crib and parked on the side of the curb. He had been trying to get a hold of him ever since the club's shooting three weeks ago. They were posed to meet up for a meeting at club Tip'z, but shit came up for the both of them, so they rescheduled.

Hideous hadn't heard from him since then.

Hideous climbed out the BMW i8 and knocked on the door. A second later, the door slowly opened, and Ms. Parker was standing there in some all-white leggings that looked painted on by the same nigga that painted Mona Lisa. Her body was damn a masterpiece.

"Boy, what the fuck you want?" She shouted over the loud music that blared from inside her house. For an older woman, Ms. Parker acted like she was in her early twenties. Young.

"Have you talked to your son?" Hideous asked, really not in the mood for her fucked up attitude. How he was feeling, she could get a bullet in the fuckin' head too.

"No, but Sarah might have. Come on in, you know where her room is. I hope this ain't about the man who came looking for you the other day."

"What man?" He asked in a serious tone and venom in his eyes.

"He didn't leave no name. All I know is yo' ass bet not had gotten my son in yo' bullshit. He just got out, and I don't want him going back or y'all trying to be gangsters."

"Damn, this muthafucka gon' make me kill her!" He said to himself as he turned and walked down to Sarah's room.

He looked back as he knocked on Sarah's door. Ms. Parker bent over cleaning up giving him a panoramic view of her peach shape pussy. "Damn! I miss that pussy," he said under his breath.

"Oh, my gaaawwwddd!" Sarah moaned.

"What the fuck!" Hideous said as he pressed his ear to the door. He reached for the doorknob and eased the door open. Under the sheets Sarah was going in with her dildo.

"Ahhhh, oh my gawwd! She moaned moving the dildo in and out of her soaked pussy. With her eyes shut, she never saw Hideous creep into her room.

Hideous watched for minute, then announced himself. He felt creepy watching her like that.

"Oh, my gawwwwd!" She cried as she opened her eyes, unaware of an audience.

Looking up into Hideous' cold eyes, she quickly shut her legs.

Hideous raised the silk sheet. She felt a little embarrassed at first but got comfortable with his presence. He always made her feel safe.

"I came over to see if you heard from yo' brother?"

"Yeah, he was supposed to take me back to school, but his bitch ass still ain't showed. I just came."

"Call him and tell him and let me talk to him."

"Okay, hold up?"

Motel 6

"It's crazy how niggas be wanting to fuck a fat ass but can't handle it. I swear I be serving y'all asses!" Susie spat, staring at Shoota Face limp dick,. He couldn't hang with her. Five minutes hitting it from the back, he bust. Truth be told, he couldn't handle all that ass, and Susie threw it back hard every time.

He was glad to see his phone going off with his sister's picture flashing on the screen, "What it do, lil one?"

"Hey, where you at?" she asked with a hint of attitude in her voice.

"Fuck! I forgot. I'm on the way," He lied. He wasn't ever going to take her. He been ducked off in the motel room for almost three weeks now with Big Booty Susie. She didn't mind long as he paid for the room and her services. His money was getting real short, but he didn't care because he still had his two whole kilos lying next to him still wrapped in plastic inside the Goyard shoulder bag.

"Bro, stop lying. Don't worry about it. I got a ride," Sarah snapped. "Hideous, do you mind taking me back to school. I'll pay you."

"That nigga over there?"

"Yeah, and he said to call him. It's an emergency."

"Fuck what he said. If you get in that car with him, I'm gon' beat the fuck outta you."

He began cussing his bitch out. "Don't you see I'm on the fuckin' phone, bitch?" He spat.

"Say, put that nigga on."

"What it do? Where you at? I need them two bricks from ya. I feel like you been ducking me."

"Look, check this out. You not getting a fuck thing. Now get yo' bitch ass up out my crib before we have a big problem."

"Who the fuck you talking too?" Hideous stared at the phone like it had shit on it. "Nigga, you for real?"

"As a heart attack."

"Bet, we gone cross paths real soon and when we do, you know what it is. Just be ready to let them thangz go, pussy."

Click!

"What happened, Reuben?" Sarah asked looking confused.

"Just know yo' brother taught me a valuable lesson."

"And what is that?"

"Never trust no one!"

With that he stood and left the room.

Once Hideous was in the car, he grabbed his iPhone from the passenger's seat and cut it on. He had messages all from different hoes. His most recent was from Caprice and Scream that was from few hours ago.

Damn, I been like that? He thought.

Caprice: I know you not with no bitch! You told Butter you were going straight to yo' sister's school. See you stay trying to play on my top.

Two minutes later.

Caprice: So, you can't text back, you can't answer the phone, bet!

Three minutes later.

Caprice: I love you!

Ten minutes apart from Caprice's message.

Scream: Oh my God! Reuben, Caprice is dead. They killed her. They killed my best friend!

Hideous had to re-read the message because for a minute he thought his eyes were playing tricks on him.

"Oh my God! Reuben, Caprice is dead. They shot her! They shot her!"

He read the message over and over until it processed in his head that Caprice was dead.

"What the fuck have I been doing that I couldn't check my phone," he said out loud.

"Rachel!" He quickly called her phone. It rang and rang. "Answer the phone, damn!" He barked, hitting the steering wheel. She finally answered on the fifth call.

"Hello, Reuben, I been calling you and calling you."

"Calm down; tell me what happened."

"I don't know, Reuben. It all happened so fast."

"Damn, where you at now?"

"Back at the school."

"Listen to me, I'm on my way. I think I know who's behind this, Sarah told me a man came looking for me."

Static. Click.

"Hello, hello!" Scream yelled looking at her phone.

CHAPTER 20

Pay Up

After Scream took a long-needed shower, she carefully rubbed lotion all over her entire body, including her round ass. She put on a large white Armani Exchange shirt that hugged her curves like a skintight dress. She picked up her phone and browsed through her Instagram. Ever since she was the cover girl for Straight Kite DM Magazine, her followers skyrocketed.

She walked into the living room where Jelly was sitting on the sofa smokin' a blunt.

"Damn, bitch what?" Jelly asked.

"Bitch, you ain't run yo' mouf to nobody right?" Scream asked.

"Please, don't start with me. I haven't told anybody, I promise," Jelly responded, knowing Scream had been watching her closely since she killed ol' boy.

Scream rolled her eyes and walked across the room to the entertainment system and pressed the play button. The sound of Trapboy Freddy blasted from the speakers and filled the room.

"I'm just saying this is between me, you, Butter, and now my brother."

"Oh my God! You told yo' brother?"

"Fuck yeah, that was his bitch that got killed."

"Damn, how did he take it?"

"Bad, he's on his way over here right now. Fuck! This is all my fault!"

"It's going to be okay. Nobody saw us enter the room with them. They just saw Caprice and Butter."

BOOM! BOOM! BOOM!

Both women looked at each other like.

"Bitch, who is that?"

She shrugged her shoulders. She didn't think it was her brother that quick.

Scream walked toward the front door and slowly crept to it.

"What if it's the police!" Jelly said putting' her hand to her mouth.

"Bitch, shut the fuck up!"

But what if it was, Scream thought.

As soon as Scream opened the door, she was welcome by two masked men who were standing there aiming handguns. On the side of the two massive men, stood another man who smiled at her.

Scream made a run for it, but Uzi Mi hands were already on her neck. He lifted her into the air and tackled her to the ground like she was an NFL running back.

"Damn, who was it. And what you doing?" Jelly words hung in thin air once she saw the two massive gunmen and a third man on top of her roommate pinning her down to the floor.

Jelly opened her mouth to scream but Black Rhino's huge hand was over her mouth before any sound could come out. She kicked and clawed at the massive man, but he secured her arms quickly to her sides.

A moment later, Uzi Mi had the two young ladies sitting on their bare asses on the linoleum tile in the kitchen, with their mouths taped shut and their wrists taped behind their backs. Their ankles were taped together and their backs rested against the stove.

"You two bitches know why I'm here. Where is my muthafuckin' money?" He asked as he squatted down in front of Scream who was sobbing uncontrollably. He ripped the tape from across her mouth. "Where the fuck is my money!" Uzi Mi asked her again.

"What money is you talking about?"

WHAM!

Uzi Mi hit her with a powerful slap to the face.

"This what's about to go down. I'm gon' have one of my niggas here fuck both of y'all in all three holes until y'all tell me where the fuck my money at."

This can't be happening, Scream thought as she looked over of at his niggas. They were well over six feet tall and weighed well over two hundred pounds, all muscle.

The bigger one of the two name was Black Rhino; he rubbed his dick while lustfully staring at Scream's exposed thighs.

Scream started shivering at the sight. "I swear I don't know what you talking about."

"Mmm! Mmmm!" Jelly screamed from behind the duct tape, shaking her head from side to side. Unlike Scream she wasn't about to die for nobody. She'll tell them whatever they wanted to know and then some.

Uzi Mi said to her, "Bitch, you know where my money is?"

Jelly nodded her head. He bent down on one knee and ripped the tape from her mouth.

"Yes, it's under her bed in a trash bag," Jelly said quickly.

"Bitch!" Scream yelled in a nasty tone, causing Uzi Mi to silence her with a solid punch to the jaw.

"I'm sorry, but I'm not about to die for you or anybody else," cried Jelly.

Uzi Mi turned to Monster B, "Go get that."

A second later, Monster B came back with a trash bag and a torn Louie V bag. He handed it to Uzi Mi who turned it over and emptied it out. Money and jewelry fell on the floor.

"What the fuck is this?"

"Yo money she got from the hotel. Ain't that's the money?" Jelly asked, voice trembling all over.

WHAM!

"Bitch! Do this like seven hunnid thousand?"

Jelly held her bloody lip as the tears flooded. She didn't have a clue what he was talking about. She was there. She watched Scream take the money, and it wasn't nowhere near that amount.

Uzi Mi grabbed his Glock from its holster and pointed it at Jelly.

"Please! I don't know where your money is. That's the money that she took the other day from the hotel. I watched her kill yo' man Moneybag TT. I swear I didn't have shit to do with any of it. Please, just let me go!" Jelly cried, wiping blood off her face.

"What the fuck this bitch talking about? Who the fuck is Moneybag TT? What kind of fuckin' name is that?" Uzi Mi growled. "Say, wake that bitch up!" He shouted.

Black Rhino poured a bottle of Coke that was sitting on top of the kitchen counter.

Scream jumped up and looked from side to side, she looked up and was looking into the barrel of a Glock, pointing right in her face.

"What the fuck! Just kill me already!"

"Bitch, where is your brother at with my money he stole from me?"

"He's on his way over here!" Jelly shouted.

"Bitch, I'm going to kill you!" Scream huffed trying to leap toward Jelly, but was punched in the face by Uzi Mi.

Uzi Mi turned to Black Rhino, "Put that bitch in the trunk and drive her to the spot in the East. Monster B and I will wait for her brother. Today is the day I get my money back."

Black Rhino picked up Scream and draped her limp body over his massive shoulders. Her T-shirt rose over her round ass. Black Rhino softly slapped her bare ass and walked out the front door. "I'm going to have a good time with you back at the spot," he mumbled.

An hour later

Jelly picked up Scream's iPhone and tried to call Hideous' number once again, getting the same result.

"He's not answering and I done called like six times already. This not like him, he always answers for his sister."

"Maybe you not even calling him, maybe you on some grimy shit, " Monster B stated.

"No y'all can trust me. My life is on the line here," Jelly said with her hands on her slim waist.

"Look out, ma. Come here," Uzi Mi called out to her.

She mean-mugged Monster B before walking over to where Uzi Mi stood. "Do you know where this nigga lay his head?"

"Mmm, I been to his mother's crib before, but I don't think he stays there."

"You know how to get there from here?"

"Of course, I been over there like two times now."

"Well, come on. You lead the way, ma."

The boy shorts Jelly wore was like a thong bunched up in her enormous ass. She swished toward the door with Uzi Mi and Monster B eyes glued on her ass as it jiggled on out the door.

CHAPTER 21

A Fuck'd up Situation

Driving up to a beautiful two-story home on an upscale street in Frisco, Jelly hopped out of the car and rang the doorbell with Uzi Mi and Monster B right on her heels.

"Jhonni, what are you doing here? I thought you was in Denton with Rachel?" Ms. Cash answered the door wearing some running shorts, white sheer top, and slippers. She was a very attractive woman.

"It's about your daughter. She did something that can possibly get herself a life sentence."

Uzi Mi cut her off quickly saying, "Damn, this house must cost a lot."

"You can say that my son bought it cash for me," she boasted

BOOM!

Monster B kicked the door off its hinges, knocking Ms. Cash to the floor.

Uzi Mi and Jelly rushed inside, walking over her sprawled out on the floor. They went straight to the rooms, tearing shit up, going through drawers and throwing shit on the floor looking for that money.

Ms. Cash was scared to death, "Please, don't hurt me," she cried.

"All I want is my money your son stole from me. That's all."

"I don't know where your money is. I swear to God. Please let me go and I won't call the police," she begged.

"If he had my money, it would be here. Where is it!" He snapped, pressing the Glock to her forehead.

"Please, please, oh my God! Please!" She cried.

A second later, Monster B and Jelly strolled out empty handed. "Nothing boss, and we checked everywhere."

Uzi Mi ran a hand down his face and let out a long sigh before hitting Ms. Cash across the head with the gun over and over until he saw blood and teeth.

Wham!

"Tell yo' son that Uzi Mi looking for him. Do you hear me? Uzi Mi!" He screamed standing over her bloody broken body. "Call the whole crew and tell them to strap up and meet me at the spot in the East. I'm 'bout to make the whole city bleed."

Jelly looked down at Ms. Cash and shook her head from side to side.

Hideous watched helplessly while his sister got kidnapped from her own apartment. He couldn't believe it; he had got there too late. He wanted to help her, but he didn't want to get the both of them killed. He didn't have a clue to how many niggas were inside the dormitory. But what they didn't know was Hideous following close behind. He followed the Escalade all the way to a small row house in East Dallas.

He watched as the muscular man snatch up his sister aggressively and carried her into the house, shutting the door behind.

Inside the house, Five YNs sat and played the Xbox on a huge 75-inch flat screen. "Hell, naw nigga, pay the fuck up!" Flyboi spat.

"Nigga, fuck you. I ain't paying you shit."

"What the fuck you lil niggas doing. If all y'all want to do is play video games, get the fuck up outta here," Black

Rhino hurled over his shoulder as he carried Scream to the back room.

"Damn, I didn't even hear that nigga come in," Flyboi joked. "Big ugly ass nigga."

Ten minutes later

Sweat dripped to Black Rhino's massive chest. He looked like a body builder from one of those Men's Fitness Magazines. He stood 6'4, two hundred and twenty pounds, solid muscle. He gripped the 70-pound dumbbell in each hand curling it 10 times with ease.

"Look out, Rhino," a voice from behind said, "Uzi Mi on his way, he said to get the strap out."

"Bet, now get yo' bitch ass up outta here!"

"Niggaa, what!" Flyboi said looking over at a yella bitch.

"Nigga! Don't ask me no damn questions. I said get the fuck out."

FLOOM!

Black Rhino hit him with a mean hook that sent Flyboi crashing to the ground, "Now what, nigga? You lil niggas gon' respect me."

Flyboi got up and took off running out the door, knocking shit over on his way out.

"Damn! My nigga why you tripping," Black asked trying to see what all the noise was about.

"Nigga, I'll knock yo' bitch ass out too. What you wanna do?"

Black made a wise decision and left out the room before shit got outta hand.

Black Rhino slammed the door and turned his attention to a confused looking Scream. She was still a bit dazed.

"Hey, pretty thing," An evil smile plastered across his face as he unbuckled his pants. When his pants hit the floor, Scream took off for the race. She ran toward the door, but Black Rhino snatched at her T-shirt ripping the thin material with ease as she quickly passed him, causing her to slam to the floor butt ass naked.

He picked her up into his massive arms. He sucked her earlobe and neck as he carried her off.

"Stop! Hold up, please stop!" she begged him with her back against the wall.

Black Rhino forcefully wrapped her legs around his waist and rubbed the tip of his large dick up and down her clit while squeezing on her juicy ass. Her eyes snapped shut as he whispered in her ear.

"Stop fighting, bitch. The more you fight, the harder its gon' be."

"Nooo, get the fuck off me!" She fought, not wanting his dick inside her.

"Bitch, you know what."

Scream squealed as Black Rhino managed to flip her frail body upside down with ease. He began to plant soft kisses on her juicy ass. She tried to fight from his touch, but his strength was abnormal. He spread her ass apart then flicked his wet sloppy tongue across her ass crack. That made her cringe. She wanted to kill him. She squirmed and twitched while Black Rhino tongue flicked up and down between her tiny pink hole.

Uzi Mi had just pulled up in front of one of his hideouts, unaware of Hideous. He was ducked off looking at everything coming in and leaving out.

"Damn, where the crew at?" Uzi Mi asked. He strolled up to the front porch with Monster B close behind.

Moans filled the air when he walked through his front door.

"Please! stop! No! PLEASE!" The five YNs were all standing near the door with their guns in hand.

Uzi Mi could hear a woman screaming, "What the fuck is going on in there, bro?"

"Black Rhino tripping, real talk," Black said. "The nigga up in there trying to rape a bitch. He done spazzed out on me and Flyboi," Black added.

"That shit ain't what it is, for real!" Flyboi spat holding his busted jaw.

Uzi Mi rushed into the room to find Black Rhino trying to bury his face between Scream's legs.

"Nigga, what the fuck is you doing? We don't move like that. We don't rape bitches."

Black Rhino shot up. All the Yns rushed inside the bedroom with their guns aimed and ready.

"My nigga, you tripping!" Uzi Mi barked, grabbing Black Rhino by the arm, "We don't get down like this."

"Get the fuck off me!" Black Rhino shoved Uzi Mi roughly in the chest knocking him to the wall.

"My nigga you tripping!" Monster B rushed Black Rhino and both men collided throwing haymakers at each other trying to knock each other heads off.

When the fight broke loose, Uzi Mi and the YNs quickly parted like the red sea.

Scream seen an opening and rushed over when no one was paying attention and punched Jelly off her feet. She began hitting the bitch over and over until one of Uzi Mi's men dragged her naked ass off her screaming and kicking

"Get the fuck off me!"

"Damn!" Black shouted just when Monster B knocked Black Rhino on his ass.

Uzi Mi jumped all over Black Rhino kicking and stomping him on the head. His head bounced off the floor like a Wilson basketball.

Once they stomped him half to death, Uzi Mi told his men to drag his ass out the spot.

When Hideous saw the same man climb out the wreck Dodge Charger the day of the robbery, he knew he had a problem on his hand. One that got his sister kidnapped and his bitch killed. At that moment, he knew what he had to do. He push started the BMW and drove off.

After a couple of days of being trapped in that small ass house, Scream had to admit Uzi Mi was getting serious money. She didn't have a clue to when her was going to come and rescue her, but she knew he would come somehow some way.

CHAPTER 22

Kill Season

Same night
11:00 p.m.

Hideous walked into his packed basement and posted up against the wall. He had just returned from the row house. He needed to come up with a plan to getting his sister back.

Hideous was in deep thought thinking of a way not to get himself or his sister killed. He inhaled the weed into his lungs as three big booty strippers grinded up and down on each other giving all the tricks that watched a hard on.

He sat there trying to put together a plan to get his sister out and unharmed when one of the stripper grabbed the other stripper's titties all aggressively. She put them juicy muthafuckas in her mouth, suckin' hard on the nipples. She then smacked her on her juicy ass while she stared at Hideous.

Hideous' dick grew hard, but it wasn't time to think about sex, he had to get his sister out that house, and fast. He looked into the stripper's eyes as she made that donkey ass of hers work full time, and just like that, he thought of the perfect plan.

"So, all we have to do is knock on the door, ask to buy some weed and you will give us each a thousand bucks?" The red bone stripper, whose name was Sabrina asked.

"Yeah, that simple."

"Hold up, why you can't do it yourself? Why pay three racks when you can do it for free?" Roxy asked.

"Do y'all want this money or what because I can easily get someone else in this bitch to do it!" Hideous shot back.

"Of course we want the money. Damn, bitch shut the fuck up and let's make this money. This shit easy. We would've been shaking ass all week for that kind of money," Sabrina vented.

"Okay, whatever, I'm just saying. I'm not trying to end up like Caprice," Roxy stated as she headed toward a red Tahoe parked next to a white Honda Civic. "Which car we taking, mine or Beauty's?" Roxy asked.

"Yours! I ain't got no gas like that in mines," Beauty said.

All three women scattered toward the Tahoe sitting on some red chrome 26's.

When Hideous made it to his whip, the Tahoe pulled up in front of him. Sabrina hopped out and swayed over to the BMW i8.

"What's the addy, nigga?"

"I'm gon' send you the location."

"Where it's at girl?" Roxy yelled over the loud music blasting through her speakers.

"East Dallas, bitch!"

Hideous closed the butterfly door to his whip and watched as they drove off, music playing loud than a bitch He was about to drive off when he noticed a white Crown Vic creeping toward him; the same one from the other night.

Not waiting for them to bust first, Hideous snatched up his Uzi from the driver seat. He raced around his whip and let his bitch go feeding off his anger.

BUDDABUDDA! BUDDABUDDA!

The bullets hit Crown Vic, filling it with tattered holes on the side.

Fat Al was in the back loading the AK-47 with gorilla nuts when suddenly the stolen Vic was struck by bullets that felt like hundreds of golf ball size hail.

He ducked his head while Lil Mike Mike stomped on the gas.

Hideous ran to the middle of the street with his Uzi going the fuck off. A barrage of bullets hit the back window shattering the windshield, causing the car to jerk. The car skidded and crashed, hitting a parked car.

Showing no remorse, Hideous walked up to the damaged vehicle just as Fat Al managed to crawl out. He was shot in the back multiple times.

Hideous stepped over Fat Al and peered his head inside the Vic. The driver was dead. The other man on the passenger side was still breathing; his chest was heaving up and down.

Hideous aimed the Uzi inside the car and filled his body with bloody holes at close range.

Hideous looked back in time to see Fat Al had crawled a good distance away, but not far enough where he could get away. He walked up on him not giving a fuck about the crowd that had come out the club and out their homes around the neighborhood.

"Who the fuck sent you?" Hideous barked, kicking Fat Al in the side so hard he was trying to break some.

"Fuck you!" Fat Al mumbled, blood spitting out his mouth.

"Wrong answer!" Hideous kicked him several more times with more force.

"Ahhhhh!" Fat Al yelled in pain. Feeling defeated, he said, "You killed my cousin Yella Kid."

"Nigga, fuck Yella Kid." Hideous aimed the Uzi at Fat Al. He was in no shape to defend himself from the hail of bullets that rained tore through his flesh.

CHAPTER 23

Ready to Die

Uzi Mi let his niggas take off to get him and Scream something to eat. She had been captive for hours now.

He had niggas out looking for her brother, and at any giving time, they could return with his head on a dinner plate.

Uzi Mi stepped into the room he had Scream in. She was standing by the window looking out at the world. She was wearing one of his designer shirts and boxers.

"Soon, your brother gives me back what he'd stolen. I will let you go. I promise I'm not here to hurt you and I'm very sorry again for what my nigga tried to do did to ya, but nothing like that will ever happen again do you hear me?" He asked, stepping so close behind her that he could smell the body wash she had on her.

Scream turned and eyeballed him, "I just want to go home. I don't have shit to do with what my brother did and what y'all got going."

"Yes, you do!" He shot back.

"What?"

"You're collateral. Long as I got you, he'll turn up."

Scream rolled her eyes. "And when he does it's not gon' be pretty. I just hope you're ready to die," she warned as she turned back to face the window.

"I hear you talking."

"What?" She hurled over her shoulder, turning to look at him again.

Lost in her hazel eyes, he had to admit she was the prettiest woman he had ever laid his eyes on, and he'd been with plenty of them.

"When he shows, I'll be ready. I just hope he'll be ready to die," he spoke, raising his designer shirt and showing off his .45 caliber Glock.

Scream looked him up and down. "You going to need more than that."

***

After killing them niggas back at his club and getting all the money out, Hideous drove toward the East. He blew out a cloud of blue smoke while his adrenaline pumped through his veins.

He had one thing on his mental and it was to kill or be killed. As he drove through the dark city streets, he smoked blunt after blunt, ready to put a bullet in anybody that crossed him. He didn't give a fuck right about now. All he wanted was his sister.

As he exited Dolphin and made that quick right, his phone rang. He picked it up. It was Sabrina fine ass, "Wassup? Where y'all at?"

"Boy, we been here for about ten minutes now waiting on you. Where you at?" She said over the loud music.

"About to pull up now. Meet me by the store across from the milk plant so I can run the play by y'all again."

After gaming the three thick chicks, Hideous sat back and lit the tip of another blunt. He inhaled deep and blew out a thick fog of smoke. It was showtime.

All three women wore short ass dresses with thigh high boots that barley covered their fat asses. Hideous watched as they climbed out the Tahoe, all three women were thick and juicy. Their asses did a fool underneath them short ass dresses. It was like watching two bumper cars going at it at the state fair.

They walked up the porch leading to the front door, arguing back and forth about who would knock.

"Bitch, this was all you who wanted to make this extra cash so bad, so you knock," Roxy said twisting her neck from side to side like a hoodrat.

"Bitch, whatever. I swear you get on my muthafuckin' nerves," Sabrina hissed as she nervously knocked on the door. All three women waited patiently for someone to answer.

A moment later, Uzi Mi snatched opened the door holding a big ass gun aimed at their faces.

"What the fuck you bitches want?"

"Hold up, you don't got to handle us like tha. All we wanted was some weed. That's it!" Sabrina let it be known not hiding her attitude. She placed her hand on her wide hips and cocked her head to the side.

Uzi Mi looked at the thick red bitch like she had just bit his dick off and swallowed it. He started to shoot her in her disrespectful mouth, but he didn't want to scare Scream more than she already was.

"Bitch, this ain't no trap house. Now, get y'all dirty asses off my porch before I kill y'all."

SLAM!

The expression on the three women's faces changed once the realization hit them when the door slammed in their faces.

On their way back to the car, Sabrina looked back. She had never got done the way she just did. Most niggas usually begged just to take her out. She saw Uzi Mi peeking' out the blinds, so she decided to give him a show. She raised the hem of her short dress and put her hands in the air and began to make her red ass cheeks clap something serious.

Roxy and Beauty laughed and followed suit. They raised their dresses up too. Uzi Mi was staring at three phat asses clapping.

"You couldn't handle all this ass no way! Sabrina hurled over her shoulder while her ass cheeks met head-on like a pay-a-view fight.

Hideous chuckled as he reached back and grabbed the duffle bag full of money. He grabbed the Uzi just in case.

He raised the door up and laughed some more when he seen Sabrina shoot up her middle finger while that ass moved non-stop.

He crouched down low and made his way toward the small row house. He looked back just in time to see Sabrina pulling down her dress as she climbed into the red Tahoe. She made an imaginary gun with her thumb and aimed it at Uzi Mi. She pulled the imaginary trigger twice, mouthing' off, "Pow! Pow!"

Uzi Mi stepped out the house gun in hand. He was about to shoot until the Tahoe burnt off into the darkness. "Scary ass bitches!" He shouted.

As soon as Uzi Mi stepped back into the house, he felt the cold steel to the back of his neck.

"I heard you been looking for me!"

While Uzi Mi was outside flashing his gun, Hideous was checking window after window until he came across one that was unlocked and slowly opened it wide enough to climb inside.

"Say, my nigga, I got to give it to you. You got some serious balls to come up in my shit unnoticed and untouched!"

"Where the fuck is my sister?" Hideous roared through clenched teeth, digging the muzzle of the gun into the back of his neck.

"She's alive."

"RACHEL!" Hideous walked around and snatched the .45 outta Uzi Mi's hand and tucked the gun in his waistline while having the Uzi trained on him.

Scream rushed into the living room. "Reuben, you came for me," she whispered.

"Is you okay?"

"Yeah!" She said with tears in her eyes.

Hideous turned his attention back to Uzi Mi and swung the Uzi like a major league baseball player, cracking Uzi Mi's head. He wasn't paying him shit. But before he knew it, they were wrestling for the gun.

"Rachel, help!"

She tried her hardest to get Uzi Mi off her brother. But he was too strong. His will to live gave him strength he didn't know he had. They both continued to tussle for the Uzi when they both heard the bitch go off.

BUDDABUDDA!

Hideous looked up and saw his sister's body jerking from side to side.

"Rachel!" He ran to her aide. He dropped to his knees and began to cry as hard as he could remember ever crying.

"Rachel, please, don't leave me like this. I'm soooo sorry!"

"You will always be my hero." she mumbled above a whisper, dying in his arms.

Hideous eyes got wide then a muthafucka. He shook his head from side to side. He didn't wanna believe she was dead.

Hideous put his head down and cried and cried. When he opened his eyes, he looked at his sister one last time. She was looking up at him. He shut her eye lids and said above a whisper. "I love you, baby girl."

When Hideous turned his head, Uzi Mi and the money were gone.

He vowed on his sister's dead body he was going to hunt down and kill Uzi Mi. Then, bring him back to life and kill him again, if that was the last thing he ever did. The killing was just the beginning.

Epilouge

Mark D. Anthony couldn't figure out what was happening. The murder rate was on the rise, one body after the next.

He visualized the scene with intense concentration.

The high yella woman looked real familiar to him. He just couldn't put her face into memory. One thing he didn't understand was; who would want to kill someone as beautiful as her?

He observed the crime scene closely. He looked at the girl again, and then it hit him.

"The girl from the fire," he remembered. His father saved her, but couldn't save her twin brother, but he still managed to get out with serious burns. A couple of weeks later, his father was pronounced dead.

"What is this bitch's name?" He said rubbing his hand over his face in frustration. Then it came to him like a bad dream in the middle of the night.

"Rachel Cash!" He remembered that last name Cash. That was the same name that witnesses were saying killed his old man in broad daylight in front of his home. "Reuben "Hideous" Cash."

"I got to find that nigga. And when I do, I'm going to put a bullet in his head."

To Be Continued...

COMING SOON

HIDEOUS 2

A Bloody Nightmare

Lock Down Publications and Ca$h Presents Assisted Publishing Packages

Due to an increase in the price of services we have increased our prices. The prices below reflect the price increase as of 11/1/24.

BASIC PACKAGE **$699** Editing Cover Design Formatting	**UPGRADED PACKAGE** **$1000** Typing Editing Cover Design Formatting Upload eBooks to Amazon Upload Paperback to Amazon
ADVANCE PACKAGE **$1,400** Typing Editing (line editing/content) Cover Design Formatting Copyright Registration Proofreading Upload eBooks to Amazon Upload Paperback to Amazon	**LDP SUPREME PACKAGE** **$1,700** Typing Editing (line editing/content) Cover Design Formatting Copyright Registration Proofreading Set up Amazon Account Upload eBooks to Amazon Upload Paperback to Amazon Advertise on LDP's Amazon and Facebook Page

***

Other services available upon request.
Additional charges may apply

Lock Down Publications
P.O. Box 944
Stockbridge, GA 30281-9998
Phone: 470 303-9761
Email: lockdownpublications@gmail.com

Submission Guideline

Submit the first three chapters of your completed manuscript to ldpsubmissions@gmail.com. In the subject line add **Your Book's Title**. The manuscript must be in a Word Doc file and sent as an attachment. Document should be in Times New Roman, double spaced, and in size 12 font. Also, provide your synopsis and full contact information. If sending multiple submissions, they must each be in a separate email.

Have a story but no way to send it electronically? You can still submit to LDP/Ca$h Presents. Send in the first three chapters, written or typed, of your completed manuscript to:

LDP: Submissions Dept
P.O. Box 944
Stockbridge, GA 30281-9998

DO NOT send original manuscript. Must be a duplicate. Provide your synopsis and a cover letter containing your full contact information.

Thanks for considering LDP and Ca$h Presents.

NEW RELEASES

BLOODLINE OF A SAVAGE 1-3
THESE VICIOUS STREETS 1-3
RELENTLESS GOON 1-3
BY PRINCE A. TAUHID

THE BUTTERFLY MAFIA 1-3
BY FUMIYA PAYNE

A THUG'S STREET PRINCESS 1&2
BY MEESHA

CITY OF SMOKE 3
BY MOLOTTI

GET IT IN SLUGS 1 &2
BY B. STALL

STANDING ON HER BUSINESS 1&2
BY DG SANTANA

STEPPERS 1,2&3
THE REAL BADDIES OF CHI-RAQ
BY KING RIO

THE LANE 1&2
BY KEN-KEN SPENCE

THUG OF SPADES 1&2
LOVE IN THE TRENCHES 2
CORNER BOYS
BY COREY ROBINSON

TIL DEATH 3
BY ARYANNA

HIDEOUS | TOMMY COOK

THE BIRTH OF A GANGSTER 4
BY DELMONT PLAYER

PRODUCT OF THE STREETS 1-3
BY DEMOND "MONEY" ANDERSON

NO TIME FOR ERROR
BY KEESE

MONEY HUNGRY DEMONS 1-2
BY TRANAY ADAMS

HUB CITY MENACE 1-3
BY J. WHITE

A THUGGISH PASSION 1&2
LAND OF DA HOOLIGANZ 1-4
KILLAZ ON STANDBY 1&2
BY IRA B.

FO'EVA ROLLIN 1&2
BY ASSA RAYMOND BAKER

THE LEVEL UP 1&3
BY LUXURY KING

Coming Soon from Lock Down Publications/Ca$h Presents

IF YOU CROSS ME ONCE 6
ANGEL V
By Anthony Fields

A THUGS STREET PRINCESS 3
By Meesha

CORNER BOYS 2
By Corey Robinson

THA TAKEOVER
By Keith Chandler

BETRAYAL OF A G 2
By Ray Vinci

SAVAGE FAMILY EMPIRE 1&2
SOULLESS GOON 1,2&3
THE DIRTY SIDE OF MONEY 1,2&3
By Prince

FOR MY ENEMY'S SAKE
AMBITIONS OF A SLIDER
FRESH OFF DA PORCH
By IRA B.

BY THE TRUCKLOAD 1-4
TIPPIN' THE SCALES 1-3
BAD BITCHES WIT GUNZ 3
PROBLEM SOLVED 2
By Christopher "Diesel" Hornezes

Available Now

RESTRAINING ORDER 1 & 2
By **CA$H & Coffee**

LOVE KNOWS NO BOUNDARIES 1-3
By **Coffee**

RAISED AS A GOON I, II, III & IV
BRED BY THE SLUMS I, II, III
BLAST FOR ME I & II
ROTTEN TO THE CORE I II III
A BRONX TALE I, II, III
DUFFLE BAG CARTEL I II III IV V VI
HEARTLESS GOON I II III IV V
A SAVAGE DOPEBOY I II
DRUG LORDS I II III
CUTTHROAT MAFIA I II
KING OF THE TRENCHES
By **Ghost**

LAY IT DOWN I & II
LAST OF A DYING BREED I II
BLOOD STAINS OF A SHOTTA I & II III
By **Jamaica**

LOYAL TO THE GAME I II III
LIFE OF SIN I, II III
By **TJ & Jelissa**

IF LOVING HIM IS WRONG…I & II
LOVE ME EVEN WHEN IT HURTS I II III
By **Jelissa**

PUSH IT TO THE LIMIT
By **Bre' Hayes**

HIDEOUS | TOMMY COOK

BLOODY COMMAS I & II
SKI MASK CARTEL I, II & III
KING OF NEW YORK I II, III IV V
RISE TO POWER I II III
COKE KINGS I II III IV V
BORN HEARTLESS I II III IV
KING OF THE TRAP I II
By **T.J. Edwards**

WHEN THE STREETS CLAP BACK I & II III
THE HEART OF A SAVAGE I II III IV
MONEY MAFIA I II
LOYAL TO THE SOIL I II III
By **Jibril Williams**

A DISTINGUISHED THUG STOLE MY HEART I II & III
LOVE SHOULDN'T HURT I II III IV
RENEGADE BOYS 1-4
PAID IN KARMA 1-3
SAVAGE STORMS 1-3
AN UNFORESEEN LOVE 1-3
BABY, I'M WINTERTIME COLD 1-3
A THUG'S STREET PRINCESS 1&2
By **Meesha**

A GANGSTER'S CODE 1-3
A GANGSTER'S SYN 1-3
THE SAVAGE LIFE 1-3
CHAINED TO THE STREETS 1-3
BLOOD ON THE MONEY 1-3
A GANGSTA'S PAIN 1-3
BEAUTIFUL LIES AND UGLY TRUTHS
CHURCH IN THESE STREETS
By **J-Blunt**

CUM FOR ME 1-8
An LDP Erotica Collaboration

BLOOD OF A BOSS 1-5
SHADOWS OF THE GAME
TRAP BASTARD
By **Askari**

THE STREETS BLEED MURDER 1-3
THE HEART OF A GANGSTA 1-3
By **Jerry Jackson**

WHEN A GOOD GIRL GOES BAD
By **Adrienne**

THE COST OF LOYALTY 1-3
By **Kweli**

BRIDE OF A HUSTLA 1-3
THE FETTI GIRLS 1-3
CORRUPTED BY A GANGSTA 1-4
BLINDED BY HIS LOVE
THE PRICE YOU PAY FOR LOVE 1-3
DOPE GIRL MAGIC 1-3
By **Destiny Skai**

A KINGPIN'S AMBITION
A KINGPIN'S AMBITION II
I MURDER FOR THE DOUGH
By **Ambitious**

TRUE SAVAGE 1-7
DOPE BOY MAGIC 1-3
MIDNIGHT CARTEL 1-3
CITY OF KINGZ 1&2
NIGHTMARE ON SILENT AVE
THE PLUG OF LIL MEXICO 1&2
CLASSIC CITY
By **Chris Green**

HIDEOUS | TOMMY COOK

A GANGSTER'S REVENGE 1-4
THE BOSS MAN'S DAUGHTERS 1-5
A SAVAGE LOVE 1&2
BAE BELONGS TO ME 1&2
A HUSTLER'S DECEIT 1-3
WHAT BAD BITCHES DO 1-3
SOUL OF A MONSTER 1-3
KILL ZONE
A DOPE BOY'S QUEEN 1-3
TIL DEATH 1-3
IMMA DIE BOUT MINE 1-6
DYING FOR LIKES
By **Aryanna**

A DOPEBOY'S PRAYER
By **Eddie "Wolf" Lee**

THE KING CARTEL 1-3
By **Frank Gresham**

THESE NIGGAS AIN'T LOYAL 1-3
By **Nikki Tee**

GANGSTA SHYT 1-3
By **CATO**

THE ULTIMATE BETRAYAL
By **Phoenix**

BOSS'N UP 1-3
By **Royal Nicole**

I LOVE YOU TO DEATH
By **Destiny J**

I RIDE FOR MY HITTA
I STILL RIDE FOR MY HITTA
By **Misty Holt**

LOVE & CHASIN' PAPER
By **Qay Crockett**

TO DIE IN VAIN
SINS OF A HUSTLA
By **ASAD**

BROOKLYN HUSTLAZ
By **Boogsy Morina**

BROOKLYN ON LOCK 1 & 2
By **Sonovia**

GANGSTA CITY
By **Teddy Duke**

A DRUG KING AND HIS DIAMOND 1-3
A DOPEMAN'S RICHES
HER MAN, MINE'S TOO 1&2
CASH MONEY HO'S
THE WIFEY I USED TO BE 1&2
PRETTY GIRLS DO NASTY THINGS
By **Nicole Goosby**

LIPSTICK KILLAH 1-3
CRIME OF PASSION 1-3
FRIEND OR FOE 1-3
By **Mimi**

TRAPHOUSE KING 1-3
KINGPIN KILLAZ 1-3
STREET KINGS 1&2
PAID IN BLOOD 1&2
CARTEL KILLAZ 1-3
DOPE GODS 1&2
By **Hood Rich**

THE STREETS ARE CALLING
By **Duquie Wilson**

STEADY MOBBN' 1-3
THE STREETS STAINED MY SOUL 1-3
By **Marcellus Allen**

WHO SHOT YA 1-3
SON OF A DOPE FIEND 1-4
HEAVEN GOT A GHETTO 1&2
SKI MASK MONEY 1&2
By **Renta**

GORILLAZ IN THE BAY 1-4
TEARS OF A GANGSTA 1/&2
3X KRAZY 1&2
STRAIGHT BEAST MODE 1&2
By **DE'KARI**

TRIGGADALE 1-3
MURDA WAS THE CASE 1-3
By **Elijah R. Freeman**

SLAUGHTER GANG 1-3
RUTHLESS HEART 1-3
By **Willie Slaughter**

GOD BLESS THE TRAPPERS 1-3
THESE SCANDALOUS STREETS 1-3
FEAR MY GANGSTA 1-5
THESE STREETS DON'T LOVE NOBODY 1-2
BURY ME A G 1-5
A GANGSTA'S EMPIRE 1-4
THE DOPEMAN'S BODYGAURD 1&2
THE REALEST KILLAZ 1-3
THE LAST OF THE OGS 1-3
By **Tranay Adams**

MARRIED TO A BOSS 1-3
By **Destiny Skai & Chris Green**

KINGZ OF THE GAME 1-7
CRIME BOSS 1-4
By **Playa Ray**

FUK SHYT
By **Blakk Diamond**

DON'T F#CK WITH MY HEART 1&2
By **Linnea**

ADDICTED TO THE DRAMA 1-3
IN THE ARM OF HIS BOSS
By **Jamila**

LOYALTY AIN'T PROMISED 1&2
By **Keith Williams**

YAYO 1-4
A SHOOTER'S AMBITION 1&2
BRED IN THE GAME
By **S. Allen**

TRAP GOD 1-3
RICH $AVAGE 1-3
MONEY IN THE GRAVE 1-3
CARTEL MONEY 1&2
By **Martell Troublesome Bolden**

FOREVER GANGSTA 1&2
GLOCKS ON SATIN SHEETS 1&2
By **Adrian Dulan**

TOE TAGZ 1-4
LEVELS TO THIS SHYT 1&2
IT'S JUST ME AND YOU
By **Ah'Million**

KINGPIN DREAMS 1-3
RAN OFF ON DA PLUG
By **Paper Boi Rari**

THE STREETS MADE ME 1-3
By **Larry D. Wright**

CONFESSIONS OF A GANGSTA 1-4
CONFESSIONS OF A JACKBOY 1-3
CONFESSIONS OF A HITMAN
CONFESSIONS OF A DOPE BOY
By **Nicholas Lock**

I'M NOTHING WITHOUT HIS LOVE
SINS OF A THUG
TO THE THUG I LOVED BEFORE
A GANGSTA SAVED XMAS
IN A HUSTLER I TRUST
By **Monet Dragun**

QUIET MONEY 1-3
THUG LIFE 1-3
EXTENDED CLIP 1&2
A GANGSTA'S PARADISE
By **Trai'Quan**

CAUGHT UP IN THE LIFE 1-3
THE STREETS NEVER LET GO 1-3
By **Robert Baptiste**

NEW TO THE GAME 1-3
MONEY, MURDER & MEMORIES 1-3
By **Malik D. Rice**

CREAM 2-3
THE STREETS WILL TALK
By **Yolanda Moore**

THE STREETS WILL NEVER CLOSE 1-3
By **K'ajji**

LIFE OF A SAVAGE 1-4
A GANGSTA'S QUR'AN 1-4
MURDA SEASON 1-3
GANGLAND CARTEL 1-3
CHI'RAQ GANGSTAS 1-4
KILLERS ON ELM STREET 1-3
JACK BOYZ N DA BRONX 1-3
A DOPEBOY'S DREAM 1-3
JACK BOYS VS DOPE BOYS 1-3
COKE GIRLZ
COKE BOYS
SOSA GANG 1&2
BRONX SAVAGES
BODYMORE KINGPINS
BLOOD OF A GOON
By **Romell Tukes**

CONCRETE KILLA 1-3
VICIOUS LOYALTY 1-3
BLOODY MONEY BAGS
By **Kingpen**

THE ULTIMATE SACRIFICE 1-6
KHADIFI
IF YOU CROSS ME ONCE 1-3
ANGEL 1-4
IN THE BLINK OF AN EYE
By **Anthony Fields**

THE LIFE OF A HOOD STAR
By **Ca$h & Rashia Wilson**

NIGHTMARES OF A HUSTLA 1-3
BLOOD AND GAMES 1&2
By **King Dream**

GHOST MOB
By **Stilloan Robinson**

HARD AND RUTHLESS 1&2
MOB TOWN 251
THE BILLIONAIRE BENTLEYS 1-3
REAL G'S MOVE IN SILENCE
By **Von Diesel**

MOB TIES 1-7
SOUL OF A HUSTLER, HEART OF A KILLER 1-3
GORILLAZ IN THE TRENCHES
OOPS CRY TOO 1&2
THE DAUGHTER OF A CARTEL BOSS
By **SayNoMore**

BODYMORE MURDERLAND 1-3
THE BIRTH OF A GANGSTER 1-4
By **Delmont Player**

FOR THE LOVE OF A BOSS 1&2
By **C. D. Blue**

KILLA KOUNTY 1-5
TENDER
By **Khufu**

MOBBED UP 1-4
THE BRICK MAN 1-5
THE COCAINE PRINCESS 1-10
STEPPERS 1-3
SUPER GREMLIN 1-4
A GANGSTA'S SON
By **King Rio**

MONEY GAME 1&2
By **Smoove Dolla**

HIDEOUS | TOMMY COOK

A GANGSTA'S KARMA 1-5
By **FLAME**

KING OF THE TRENCHES 1-3
By **GHOST & TRANAY ADAMS**

BAD BITCHES WIT GUNZ 1&2
PROBLEM SOLVED
By "Christopher Diesel" Hornezes

QUEEN OF THE ZOO 1&2
By **Black Migo**

GRIMEY WAYS 1-3
BETRAYAL OF A G
By **Ray Vinci**

XMAS WITH AN ATL SHOOTER
By **Ca$h & Destiny Skai**

KING KILLA 1&2
By **Vincent "Vitto" Holloway**

BETRAYAL OF A THUG 1&2
By **Fre$h**

COUNTDOWN OF A KILLA 1&2
SEX, MURDER AND GOD 1&2
GUNS DOWN, BOTTOMS UP 1&2
By Lo-Life

THE MURDER QUEENS 1-7
By **Michael Gallon**

FOR THE LOVE OF BLOOD 1-4
By **Jamel Mitchell**

HIDEOUS | TOMMY COOK

HOOD CONSIGLIERE 1&2
NO TIME FOR ERROR
By **Keese**

PROTÉGÉ OF A LEGEND 1,2&3
LOVE IN THE TRENCHES 1&2
By **Corey Robinson**

THE PLUG'S RUTHLESS DAUGHTER 1&2
By **Tony Daniels**

BORN IN THE GRAVE 1-3
CRIME PAYS
By **Self Made Tay**

MOAN IN MY MOUTH
By **XTASY**

TORN BETWEEN A GANGSTER AND A GENTLEMAN
By **J-BLUNT & Miss Kim**

LOYALTY IS EVERYTHING 1-3
CITY OF SMOKE 1-3
By **Molotti**

HERE TODAY GONE TOMORROW 1&2
By **Fly Rock**

WOMEN LIE MEN LIE 1-4
FIFTY SHADES OF SNOW 1-3
STACK BEFORE YOU SPLURGE
GIRLS FALL LIKE DOMINOES
NAÏVE TO THE STREETS
By **ROY MILLIGAN**

PILLOW PRINCESS
By **S. Hawkins**

HIDEOUS | TOMMY COOK

THE BUTTERFLY MAFIA 1-3
SALUTE MY SAVAGERY 1&2
By **Fumiya Payne**

THE LANE 1&2
By Ken-Ken Spence

THE PUSSY TRAP 1-5
By **Nene Capri**

DIRTY DNA
By **Blaque**

SANCTIFIED AND HORNY
by **XTASY**

BOOKS BY LDP'S CEO, CA$H

TRUST IN NO MAN
TRUST IN NO MAN 2
TRUST IN NO MAN 3
BONDED BY BLOOD
SHORTY GOT A THUG
THUGS CRY
THUGS CRY 2
THUGS CRY 3
TRUST NO BITCH
TRUST NO BITCH 2
TRUST NO BITCH 3
TIL MY CASKET DROPS
RESTRAINING ORDER
RESTRAINING ORDER 2
IN LOVE WITH A CONVICT
LIFE OF A HOOD STAR
XMAS WITH AN ATL SHOOTER

www.ingramcontent.com/pod-product-compliance
Lightning Source LLC
LaVergne TN
LVHW010918110826
845149LV00013B/2412

9781971770130